Brady's here. Brady's here. Brady's here.

It was a chant in her head and it made her want to drive off into the sunset without a word to anyone. Never to return and have to reveal the truth. Not to her family. And certainly not to Brady Brown.

But Kate couldn't do that and she knew it. She was going to have to go out there and look him in the eye again. And pretend she wasn't more confused, more scared than she'd ever been in her life.

"You have to go out there," she told her image in the mirror. "You don't have a choice."

But maybe it wouldn't be so bad, she tried to convince herself. With her family around, he would hardly know she was there. He probably wouldn't even have a thought about their rash wedding or what had followed.

And he also wouldn't have the slightest inkling that at this very moment she was pregnant with his baby.

A RANCHING FAMILY:
Though scattered by years and tears, they share mile-deep roots in one Wyoming ranch and a singular talent for lassoing the unlikeliest hearts!

Dear Reader,

When Patricia Kay was a child, she could be found hiding somewhere…reading. "Ever since I was old enough to realize someone wrote books and they didn't just magically appear, I dreamed of writing," she says. And this month Special Edition is proud to publish Patricia's twenty-second novel, *The Millionaire and the Mom,* the next of the STOCKWELLS OF TEXAS series. She admits it isn't always easy keeping her ideas and her writing fresh. What helps, she says, is "nonwriting" activities, such as singing in her church choir, swimming, taking long walks, going to the movies and traveling. "Staying well-rounded keeps me excited about writing," she says.

We have plenty of other fresh stories to offer this month. After finding herself in the midst of an armed robbery with a gun to her back in Christie Ridgway's *From This Day Forward,* Annie Smith vows to chase her dreams…. In the next of A RANCHING FAMILY series by Victoria Pade, Kate McDermot returns from Vegas unexpectedly married and with a *Cowboy's Baby* in her belly! And Sally Tyler Hayes's *Magic in a Jelly Jar* is what young Luke Morgan hopes for by saving his teeth in a jelly jar…because he thinks that his dentist is the tooth fairy and can grant him one wish: a mother! Also, don't miss the surprising twists in *Her Mysterious Houseguest* by Jane Toombs, and an exciting forbidden love story with Barbara Benedict's *Solution: Marriage.*

At Special Edition, fresh, innovative books are our passion. We hope you enjoy them all.

Best,

Karen Taylor Richman
Senior Editor

Please address questions and book requests to:
Silhouette Reader Service
U.S.: 3010 Walden Ave., P.O. Box 1325, Buffalo, NY 14269
Canadian: P.O. Box 609, Fort Erie, Ont. L2A 5X3

Cowboy's Baby
VICTORIA PADE

SPECIAL EDITION™

Published by Silhouette Books

America's Publisher of Contemporary Romance

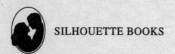 SILHOUETTE BOOKS

ISBN 0-373-24389-8

COWBOY'S BABY

Copyright © 2001 by Victoria Pade

Visit Silhouette at www.eHarlequin.com

Printed in U.S.A.

Books by Victoria Pade

Silhouette Special Edition

Breaking Every Rule #402
Divine Decadence #473
Shades and Shadows #502
Shelter from the Storm #527
Twice Shy #558
Something Special #600
Out on a Limb #629
The Right Time #689
Over Easy #710
Amazing Gracie #752
Hello Again #778
Unmarried with Children #852
Cowboy's Kin #923
Baby My Baby #946
Cowboy's Kiss #970
Mom for Hire #1057
Cowboy's Lady #1106
Cowboy's Love #1159
The Cowboy's Ideal Wife #1185
Baby Love #1249
Cowboy's Caress #1311
The Cowboy's Gift-Wrapped Bride #1365
Cowboy's Baby #1389

*A Ranching Family

Silhouette Books

Montana Mavericks:
Wed in Whitehorn
The Marriage Bargain

VICTORIA PADE

is a bestselling author of both historical and contemporary romance fiction, and mother of two energetic daughters, Cori and Erin. Although she enjoys her chosen career as a novelist, she occasionally laments that she has never traveled farther from her Colorado home than Disneyland, instead spending all her spare time plugging away at her computer. She takes breaks from writing by indulging in her favorite hobby—eating chocolate.

Printed in U.S.A.

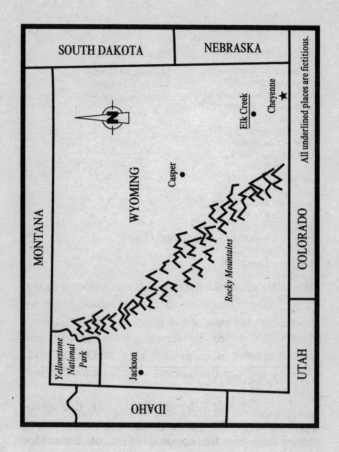

SOUTH DAKOTA

NEBRASKA

Elk Creek

Cheyenne ★

All underlined places are fictitious.

WYOMING

Casper

MONTANA

Rocky Mountains

COLORADO

Yellowstone National Park

Jackson

UTAH

IDAHO

Chapter One

Most of the McDermot family was gathered in the living room when the roar of an airplane flying so low over the house made it impossible for normal voices to be heard. Conversation halted and all eyes turned upward as an excited Matt McDermot said, "That's gotta be Brady. Four o'clock on the dot, just like he said."

Matt's expression showed his pleasure. But the arrival of her brother's old college roommate and best friend had just the opposite effect on Kate McDermot. She felt a wave of pure panic.

"Where are you going?" her brother demanded when she stood suddenly to leave the room.

"I thought I might take a little nap before dinner," she lied.

"Now? Just when Brady's gettin' here? Don't do that. I told him to land in the north field and I'm going out to pick him up right this minute. I'll have him back here before you know it and you'll want to see him, won't you?"

Not really, she was inclined to say. In fact, not at all. Brady Brown happened to be the last person on the face of the earth she wanted to see.

But she couldn't say that, so instead she said, "Sure. But maybe I'll just freshen up first."

Then she made a subtle dash to her suite of rooms, closed the door tightly behind her and leaned against it for added measure.

As if that would help.

But unfortunately it was only a stopgap measure, and she knew it. Eventually she was going to have to face Brady Brown whether she liked it or not.

Her family didn't know how she felt. They didn't know any of what had happened between her and Brady Brown. They didn't know anything about what was going on now.

But plenty *had* happened.

And there was plenty going on now.

To Kate's dismay.

She'd moved to the small Wyoming town of Elk Creek at Christmastime to live on the ranch she and her four brothers had owned since their grandfather had turned it over to them. She'd needed a change of scenery. A change of lifestyle. A change all the way around.

If only she'd made the move and let it go at that.

But after a Christmas during which her brother Matt had become engaged to a woman named Jenn Johnson, who he'd found in a snowstorm on the side of the road, Matt had talked his brothers and sister into a trip to Las Vegas. He was to meet up with Brady to celebrate their mutual thirtieth birthdays on New Year's Eve.

Kate had been reluctant to go.

Taking off on the spur of the moment, without making plans, to a place like Las Vegas, wasn't something the ultraconservative accountant usually did. But she'd been in a pretty bad funk, and in an effort to lift her spirits all of her brothers had put pressure on her to go.

So, more to humor them than anything else, she'd let herself be persuaded.

Of course, only after she'd arrived in Las Vegas had she realized that Matt had an ulterior motive. He was fixing her up with Brady Brown. And since all four of her brothers were paired off with their wives or soon-to-be wives, it was impossible for Kate and the also solo Brady not to be thrown together as a couple.

Luckily—or maybe not so luckily—Brady had made things easy on her. She was reasonably sure the cowboy crop duster hadn't had any advance warning that he was going to have Matt's sister on his hands, but he'd been great about it. Fun, funny, charming, courtly. Kate had found herself having a surprisingly good time in spite of the impromptu arrangements and being with a man she'd heard of but never met before.

But the truth of it was that she'd had *too* good a time.

New Year's Eve. Two birthdays. A lot of champagne. Being left alone with Brady after everyone else had gone off to celebrate privately in their own rooms. Las Vegas lunacy. And something that had run deeper in Kate. Much, much deeper...

At a time in her life when old feelings of being undesirable, unappealing and unattractive had resurfaced with a vengeance, Brady Brown had made her feel very desirable, very appealing, very attractive.

And the impact of even a false sense of being desirable, appealing and attractive to a jaw-droppingly handsome man who made heads turn when he walked into even the most crowded room was nothing to sneeze at. Especially in addition to way, way too much champagne. It had all gone to her head.

So when passion had erupted between them and Kate had confided her deepest secret to Brady—that she was still a virgin at twenty-nine and was fed up with saving herself for a marriage that never materialized—inebriated reasoning had somehow made it seem like a good idea for him to whisk her off to a wedding chapel at the stroke of midnight where an Elvis impersonator had performed the ceremony that gave permission to relinquish her virginity in a night of abandon that she barely remembered the next morning.

The next morning...

Kate couldn't think about that next morning without cringing.

Married. She'd actually gotten married, she shrieked silently, pushing away from the door and beginning to pace, because thoughts of what she'd gotten herself into left her too agitated to stand still any longer.

The whole thing seemed unreal.

But then, how could a person take a ceremony seriously when it was performed by an Elvis impersonator? Plus, she'd had so much to drink beforehand that everything had had a fuzzy glow to it.

But fuzzy glow or no fuzzy glow, the wedding had been real and the marriage certificate on the hotel room's bureau had proved it.

She hadn't been gracious about it. Which was part of why the memory of that next morning made her cringe. And part of why she didn't want to face Brady again.

She'd behaved pretty abominably. She'd let him know in no uncertain terms that if their marriage was real and legally binding it needed to be unbound. In a hurry.

Brady had agreed. He'd even been nice about it. He'd tried to calm her down. To make her see it in a lighter vein. To infuse a little humor into the situation.

But Kate had been having none of *that*.

It was a horrible, horrible thing they'd done, she'd told him. An incomprehensible, unconscionable thing. A completely irresponsible, foolish, foolhardy, immature, stupid thing. And it needed to be rectified immediately.

Brady had given up his attempts to reason with her or put things into a different perspective. He'd finally just assured her he would take care of it. He'd even conceded to her insistence that they not let Matt or any of her other brothers know what they'd done.

"Just relax. It'll be okay," he'd said. "I'll have the marriage dissolved one way or another."

Those were the last words he'd spoken to her before Kate had slipped out of his hotel room, sneaked back into her own room across the hall and pretended to have the flu for the remaining day of the trip so she didn't have to see Brady again.

And that had been the end of it. At least the end of any time she'd had to spend with him. Or so she'd thought. Until now.

A week ago she'd received a plain, type-written envelope containing a note from him informing her he would have divorce papers for her to sign when he got to the ranch for the visit she hadn't known he was about to make.

And since then she'd learned that seeing him again wasn't her only problem.

The thought of just how complicated things were suddenly deflated Kate. She sat on the edge of her bed and sighed a sigh that was really more of a groan.

For what seemed like the millionth time she asked herself how she could have gotten into this predicament. After all, she was the most careful person she knew. In every way. Careful, cautious, conservative. She never took a wrong step because she never took a step without thinking about it ahead of time. Without analyzing it. Without judging it from all angles first.

She drove a plain, practical sedan. She saved her money. She had a retirement plan. She wore muted colors and high necks and flat-heeled shoes and heavy coats in winter and sunblock in summer. She didn't speak out of turn. She ate in moderation. She exercised. Her whole life had been in order.

Well, it had been until Thanksgiving, anyway, when her longtime fiancé, Dwight, had pulled the rug out from under her by eloping with someone else. But even then she'd still tried to keep her life as neat and tidy as possible. She'd worked hard to keep her devastated emotions under control and undercover. And she'd given long thought to moving to Elk Creek before she'd made her decision to actually do it.

But then in one single night she'd completely blown it. All that order. All that control. All that conservatism and caution. Out the window.

"Shouldn't I have been allowed just one indiscretion without paying for it like this?" she asked the unseen forces that seemed at work in her life now.

And even if she had to pay for that one night of indiscretion, why did the payment have to be so steep? It just wasn't fair.

"Brady's here!"

Kate heard someone make that announcement in

the distance right then, and tension renewed itself and turned into needles prickling along the surface of her skin. So much so that sitting still suddenly became impossible for her.

She lunged to her feet and started pacing the room once more.

Brady's here. Brady's here. Brady's here...

It was a chant in her head, and it made her want to run away. It made her want to just get in her practical sedan and drive off into the March sunset without a word to anyone. Never to return and have to reveal what was really going on with her. To anyone. Certainly not to her family. And certainly not to Brady Brown.

But she couldn't do that and she knew it. She couldn't even stay in her bedroom hiding out from everyone. From him. She was going to have to go out there and look him in the eye again. And pretend she wasn't more confused, more scared, more worried, more muddled than she'd ever been in her life.

Good luck....

"Kate? Are you comin' out? You didn't fall asleep in there, did you?" Matt called through her door.

"I'll be right there," she answered, hoping her brother didn't hear the uncertainty in her voice.

She straightened her posture in hopes that a stiff spine might lend her courage, and took a look at herself in the mirror on the dresser.

The clothes she had on were okay—jeans and a heavy-gauge mock-turtleneck sweater with a single diamond knit into the front. But her face was so pale.

She pinched the high crests of her cheekbones until they turned color but that didn't help the wide, deer-caught-in-headlights look of her light green eyes.

"Buck up," she ordered her reflection as she ran a brush through her chin-length, riotously curly brown hair pulled back with a headband.

Then she applied a light shade of lipstick and massaged some lotion into her hands and up her arms to her elbows in hopes that that would help alleviate some of the skin-prickling tension that was still attacking her.

"You have to go out there," she told her image in the mirror as she did. "You don't have a choice."

But maybe it wouldn't be so bad, she tried to convince herself, picturing in her mind how the next several hours were likely to play out.

She would slip into the living room and say a simple hello from the sidelines—which was also where she would stay.

Brady would be involved with Matt, catching up, trading stories. He would probably hardly know she was anywhere around. He definitely wouldn't whip out the divorce papers in the middle of her whole family and demand that she sign them on the spot.

They would all have dinner and she'd keep herself as busy in the kitchen as she could so she wouldn't have to spend too much time in the same room with Brady. Then the evening would end and he'd go off to his rooms and she'd go off to hers and that would be that. He probably wouldn't even have a thought about their rash wedding or what had followed it.

And he also wouldn't have the slightest inkling of what she'd found out only four days earlier.

That the consequence of their single night of abandon was that at this very moment she was pregnant with his baby.

Chapter Two

Everyone in the living room was laughing when Kate finally ventured back there. She was only guessing, but she assumed they were laughing at something Brady had said. He could tell a joke as well as any professional comedian, which had made him the life of the party the whole time they'd all been in Las Vegas two months before.

Her family was so caught up in him, in fact, that no one noticed her standing in the arched entry from the foyer, and it gave her a chance to take a look at him.

How could he be more handsome than she remembered?

But he was.

He was as tall as her brothers—at least six foot

three. A tower of long legs, narrow hips, flat stomach, wide chest, broad shoulders and big biceps.

There wasn't an ounce of fat on him, but there were muscles galore. Muscles his clothes couldn't hide. Especially since he was wearing jeans tight enough to show off his great thighs, and a long-sleeved knit shirt that hugged his perfectly veed torso like shrink-wrap.

And as if the body wasn't enough to give her heart palpitations, he had a face to die for, too.

He had swarthy good looks. His hair was the color of French roast coffee beans—not quite coal-black but close. He wore it just a touch long and combed it with a hint of a part on the right side, sweeping all of it casually away from his face.

His skin had a natural tan to it, a golden glow that would brown up in the summer but merely gave him the look of robust health and vitality now.

And there were his features to top it all off.

Oh, he was gorgeous!

But not pretty-boy cute. He had a masculine, rugged, almost craggy kind of beauty that said he was born that way and didn't do anything to accentuate it.

His chin was strong and well defined, his lips turned up at the corners as if he were in perpetual good humor. His nose was straight and perfect, his eyebrows slightly full, and his eyes were a pale blue-gray beneath long lashes.

And when he smiled the way he did right then, there were creases that animated his face. Creases that hammocked his chin from dimples in his cheeks, creases that crinkled the corners of those eyes that glimmered with vibrancy, creases that bracketed that lissome mouth full of blindingly white teeth.

It all made for a powerful package. Powerful enough not to help the muddle Kate was already in and making something flutter inside her that had nothing to do with the baby she was carrying and everything to do with that baby's daddy and the pure animal magnetism he exuded.

A magnetism that made her step farther into the room even as another part of her wanted to run in the opposite direction just so she could get things under control.

"There she is!" Matt said from the center of the group when he spotted her. "We thought you'd gotten lost."

She had. For a moment. In the sight of Brady Brown.

But now she struggled to find her way back to some semblance of normalcy so she could play the charade she needed to play to keep her secrets.

"Say hello to Brady," her brother urged.

"Hello, Brady," she parroted, trying to make a joke out of the obvious return of Matt's overt matchmaking attempts.

But there was no joke in that first moment Brady's eyes rested on her.

Her heart started to beat double time, she felt her face flush, and although her skin still felt prickly, it didn't seem to originate in tension anymore but in something entirely different.

"Hi, Kate," Brady said in the lush baritone voice she'd forgotten about. His tone was edged with formality, though. A formality she thought might indicate he was leery of her.

But then why wouldn't he be leery of her after the way she'd treated him New Year's morning?

"Brady was just telling us about being stranded in a one-runway airport in the middle of nowhere for the past twenty-four hours," Matt said to update Kate.

"Which is why I need a shower before keepin' company with civilized people," Brady added, directing the comment at Kate. "How 'bout you show me where you folks want me to bunk? Let me clean up some?"

Kate's pulse redoubled at the prospect, even as she wondered why he didn't have Matt show him to his rooms.

But she couldn't be rude and deny a guest his request, so she forced a small smile she hoped looked better than it felt and said, "Sure."

Brady poked his chin in the direction of the front door. "My bags are there. Just let me grab 'em, and you can lead the way."

Kate saw Matt nudge her other brother Ry with an elbow and knew Matt was feeling pleased with himself, thinking that he was in the midst of a second chance at getting Kate and Brady together.

If only you knew how much trouble you've

caused, Kate thought. But she turned and retraced her steps out of the living room rather than saying anything.

Brady followed behind as Matt called after them. "We thought we'd put 'im in the rooms next to yours, Kate. Junebug got 'em all ready."

Terrific. This just gets better and better.

The house had two wings on either side of the central portion where the living room, dining room and kitchen were lined up. Both wings contained bedroom suites that allowed for privacy no matter how many of the McDermots were in residence.

The suites all had their own bedroom, bathroom and sitting room, complete with fireplaces, wet bars and French doors that allowed entrance from or exit onto the porch that wrapped around the front and sides of the place.

There was also a den and a recreation room, but Kate didn't want to prolong her time with Brady enough to give him the whole tour, so she merely took him down the hall to the right of the entrance. She went past her own door to the one beside it without saying a word, until they'd reached the entrance to the guest room Brady would be using.

"There you go," she said simply, opening the door for him but not stepping inside.

Brady craned his neck just enough to peer through the opening before he tossed in his duffel bag and slid his suitcase after it. Then he turned toward Kate, but his gaze didn't drop to her face until after he'd glanced over her head, as if to be certain they were alone in the hallway.

"I wanted to have a minute with you right away to let you know I'll be discreet about everything," he said then. "In case you were worried that I might blurt out something."

"I wasn't worried. About that," she added under her breath.

A small frown tugged at his dark brows. "Are you okay?"

"Of course. Why wouldn't I be okay? Don't I look okay?" She was too quick to answer and she regretted it.

"You look great," he said as if he meant it. "But you don't look happy to see me."

Which wasn't very hospitable. And he was being more than polite. There was thoughtfulness in his effort to reassure her he'd be keeping their secret.

Kate took a deep breath and called upon her own manners. "I'm sorry. I didn't mean to be a shrew. This whole thing is just—"

"Weird. Uncomfortable. Embarrassing. I know. It is for me, too."

It was odd, but knowing that, knowing he not only understood how she felt but was feeling the same things—well some of the same things, anyway— helped. It was comforting. Like having a comrade in arms.

"What do you say we start over?" he suggested then. "Wipe the slate clean of Las Vegas and of everything up to this minute and pretend we've just met?''

Oh, if only it were that easy.

But nothing was made any easier by her being contrary or nasty so what was the point? Especially when there was so much more they were going to have to deal with than he knew yet.

She held out her hand to him. "Hi. I'm Kate McDermot. Matt's sister. Happy to meet you."

Brady chuckled a little and accepted her hand to shake.

Not the best idea in the world.

Because only when that big callused mitt closed around hers did she recall what truly wonderful hands he had. Strong, adept, powerful, commanding. And with a touch that felt like kid leather. A touch she suddenly remembered feeling on other parts of her body and liking much too much.

"Friends?" he said then, still holding her hand and apparently having no idea what it was doing to her.

"Friends," she confirmed through a constricted throat.

Then he let go, and Kate told herself to breathe again, to act normal, to ignore the fact that that one touch had made her blood run faster in her veins.

"You wanted to shower," she reminded, since he was still just standing there, still giving her the once-over.

"Right."

"There should be towels in the cupboard in your

bathroom and fresh soap in the dish. The wet bar is probably stocked—feel free to help yourself. If you need anything else just holler."

"Thanks. I'm sure I'll be fine."

"Then I guess I'll just see you at dinner. With everyone else," she said, wondering if her cheeriness sounded as false to him as it did to her.

She finally managed to take a few steps backward, and as she did he said, "It's good to see you again, Kate."

"You, too," she answered mechanically.

Then she gave him a little wave and hightailed it back to her own rooms where she again closed herself in and leaned against the door.

Only this time she needed to wait for everything Brady Brown had put into motion inside her to settle down—her pulse, the blood racing through her veins, the prickles on her skin, the warmth where his hand had held hers....

This wouldn't do, she told herself firmly. It just wouldn't do to be susceptible to the man. She had to keep a level head and view this situation from a practical standpoint. She'd veered off the straight and narrow with Brady once, and look at how much trouble she'd gotten into. She wasn't going to let it happen again. Regardless of how great looking he was or how charming or how nice or how sexy.

No sir. Not her. Never again.

Not if it was the last thing she ever did.

But as she pushed away from the door with the strength of her determination not to let Brady have any effect on her, she realized that even if it wasn't the last thing she ever did, it just might be the most difficult.

Brady unpacked a few things, shucked the clothes he'd been wearing too long now and headed for the shower.

Matt had a nice place here, he thought as he went from the bedroom that was as big as a studio apartment into a bathroom luxurious enough to have been in a four-star hotel.

Yep, a nice place all right. A nice place filled with nice people.

So far it seemed as though his friend's idea that he check out Elk Creek for some property to invest in was a good one. Which was part of why he was there—to see the spreads Matt had called him about.

And none too soon.

Matt had told him that three different ranches were either up for sale or had owners who were making noises about selling, just when Brady had been looking for an excuse to get up here. Just when he'd been looking for something that he could use as a cover for his other reason for coming.

He needed to have Kate McDermot sign the divorce papers that would dissolve their marriage.

Their *marriage*. It shouldn't be called that. It wasn't a marriage, after all. At least not in any way that counted.

What it was was the most insane thing he'd ever done in his life.

He still couldn't believe he'd actually *married* her.

But then, he'd been in a crazy state of mind, he recalled as he stepped into the steamy spray of the shower.

Of course, he hadn't realized he'd been in a crazy state of mind at the time. In fact, he'd thought he was over the craziness that had struck after his breakup with Claudia. After all, they hadn't been married. They'd only been living together. And not for long. Sure, he'd known his pride was still bruised from her walking out on him, but he'd really thought he'd gotten past everything else.

And even the bruised pride had felt on the mend the longer he'd been with Kate in Vegas.

That had come as a surprise to him. But then, having a good time with her had come as a surprise to him, too.

Brady had known within fifteen minutes of meeting up with Matt and his family that his old college roommate had a fix-up up his sleeve. To tell the truth, Brady had been initially PO'd about it. A fix-up with his best friend's sister? That was just asking for trouble as far as Brady was concerned. It was a no-win situation.

Then he'd met Kate.

He'd liked everything about her on sight. She was more beautiful than she seemed to realize, with that buttermilk skin and those huge eyes the color of kiwi fruit.

Her mouth was lush, and she had high cheekbones

any supermodel would envy, plus curly hair that danced around a face as perfect as a Greek goddess.

And then there was that compact body with those great breasts that were just the right size....

Oh, yeah, one look at her and he'd gone from PO'd to thinking it might not be so bad to spend some time with her. As long as he kept everything light and friendly and aboveboard. What harm could it do to escort her here and there? he'd asked himself. And the answer he'd come up with was: no harm at all. A few days of enjoying her company and making Matt happy, then they'd go their separate ways.

For a while he'd thought he was pulling that off, too. He'd just been having fun, looking forward to meeting Kate at breakfast every morning and filling the rest of the day and evening with gambling or sight-seeing or shopping or taking in a show together.

Then little things had begun to strike him.

Like how sweet she could be. How nice. Like how much more fun he had when he was with her than when he wasn't. Like the fact that she had the most terrific laugh that came out sounding like wind chimes and turned her from terrific looking to stunning and made a sparkle come into her eyes that could light up a whole room.

And then it was New Year's Eve.

His and Matt's birthdays.

And then there he'd been, with his best friend and his best friend's family, with Kate, having one of the best times he'd ever had. Which had included a record number of toasts with plenty of champagne—not his drink of choice but it had been poured like water that night. And the result of everything put together was that he'd gotten carried away.

Okay, so taking Matt's sister to a wedding chapel and marrying her on the spur of the moment probably qualified as more than just getting carried away.

But that's where the insanity part had kicked in again.

By then he'd been aware that he was attracted to Kate. But maybe not how much. And if she'd been another woman he would have just tried coaxing her into spending the night with him.

But she hadn't been another woman. She was Kate. Sweet Kate. Matt's little sister. And a virgin.

Brady still didn't know how she'd arrived at twenty-nine years old with her virginity intact. Or why. But when she'd confided in him that she was a virgin, he'd known he couldn't just make love to her because they'd both been so inclined. There had to be more to it than that. It had to be special. It had to be ceremonious.

And what had his liquor-soaked brain come up with?

Marriage. They should get married....

Brady stood under the pelting spray of the showerhead and let it beat down on his face as if it might wash away the stupidity in that reasoning from two months ago.

But it didn't help. What else but *stupid* could you

call marrying your best friend's virgin sister and then taking her to bed?

Monumentally stupid.

Especially when that sister woke up the next morning feeling about it the way Kate had.

What a rude awakening that had been!

Before he'd so much as thought about what they'd done, she'd been out of bed, frantic and ordering him to rectify it.

Sure he agreed what they'd done had been dumb. But did she have to be so appalled? So outraged? So downright repulsed?

His pride hadn't just taken another strike, it had taken a full body blow—and then a knee to the groin when she'd gone on to let him know she was so horrified by having married him and slept with him, that he had to promise never to tell her brothers.

Of course, telling her brothers was not high on his top-ten list of things to do, either. But again, it wasn't an ego booster to know the extent to which Kate was disgusted by the whole situation.

That was about when he'd decided he wanted to kick himself for having fooled around with her in the first place. For having put his friendship with Matt in jeopardy. For not having seen ahead of time that Kate wasn't anywhere near as attracted to him as he'd been to her.

And rebruised pride or no rebruised pride, Brady hadn't been left with a doubt in his mind that the best thing for everyone was to do exactly what Kate had ordered him to do just before she'd run out of the room as if she couldn't stand to spend another minute with him—dissolve the marriage.

Which was what he had contacted a lawyer for the very next day.

So now, as soon as she signed the papers and they filed them, it would finally be over and they could put it behind them. Once and for all.

Finished with his shower, Brady got out of the stall and wrapped a towel around his waist. Then he used another towel to clear the mirror to shave.

As he did, he couldn't help wondering if, when he could put this fiasco behind him, he would also be able to get Kate McDermot off his mind.

Because that's where she had been for the past two months. Stubbornly, continuously, vividly on his mind. No matter what he tried to do to dislodge her.

But would some simple paperwork accomplish that? Especially when seeing her again had done what it had done to him?

Even surrounded by her family and at a distance, he'd still felt her presence the very instant she'd walked into the living room. It had been as if the temperature had suddenly risen. As if everything were brighter. As if all the colors around him were more vivid.

And that was before he'd so much as glanced at her.

Then he'd looked up and seen her for the first time since New Year's morning, and he'd been struck all over again by how beautiful she was in that quietly understated way of hers. With those sparkling green eyes and that wildly curly honey-brown hair shot through with streaks of gold, and those tender lips he remembered kissing until they'd grown puffy....

Damn if he hadn't wanted to walk away from the rest of her family and go to her, take her in his arms, kiss her again the way he had that night....

Brady nicked himself with his razor, drawing blood.

"That's what you get for thinking those kinds of things," he told himself as he tore a corner from a tissue and pressed it to the wound.

And why the hell was he thinking about this now?

He'd already made one huge mistake with that woman and she'd let him know what she thought of him for it.

So what good did it do to be wallowing in this damn attraction to her?

No good, that's what.

"So shake it off," he ordered.

And that's exactly what he was going to do.

Even though a part of him was itching to do something entirely different. To do a little courting. A little charming. A little wooing...

But that was the stupid, crazy part of him.

Because if there was one thing he'd learned in the past year—and learned the hard way—it was that no amount of tenacity or persistence, no amount of wooing or wining and dining or gift giving, could change a woman's feelings once she'd decided she didn't want him.

And Kate McDermot had made it more than clear

the morning after their wedding that she didn't want him. Or anything to do with him.

So he was here to visit Matt, to look at some property, to get the divorce papers signed, and that was it.

And if Kate McDermot could still rock his world just by walking into a room? Too bad.

He wasn't giving in to the attraction. He wasn't letting it put him in any position where he could be dealt another emotional body blow the way Claudia had done.

And if he and Kate had had one incredible night together? Obviously it hadn't been as incredible for her as it had been for him.

So that one night was all they were ever going to have together. Because he just didn't need any more grief.

And that's all there was to it.

Chapter Three

"Go on in with your company," Junebug Brimley told Kate, making a shooing motion with her hands in the direction of the door that led from the kitchen to the dining room.

Junebug was the McDermots' housekeeper. All six feet, three hundred pounds of her.

"I want to help," Kate informed her, trying to do what she'd decided to do to get through dinner that evening—make herself as scarce as possible by staying in the kitchen.

"Don't need your help," the booming-voiced woman told her bluntly. "Raised a passel of sons who ate like bears comin' out of hibernation at every meal. I think I can put on this dinner without too much strain."

"But we're all here tonight," Kate reminded her.

All being those family members who lived in the big house built to accommodate them—her twin brothers Ry and Shane, their wives, Tallie and Maya, and Ry's nearly three-year-old son, Andrew, Matt, Jenn and Kate, along with Bax—Elk Creek's doctor who lived in town—and his wife Carly and his going-on-seven-year-old daughter, Evie Lee, plus Brady.

"All or not, I can do it myself," Junebug said, holding firm. "You're missin' time with Matt's friend in there."

"That's just it—he's Matt's friend. Not mine. I don't have anything to say to him."

"I heard the two of you liked each other fine in Las Vegas," Junebug said slyly.

"He's a nice enough man. But that was then, and this is now, and he's here to visit Matt, not me."

Junebug eyed Kate as if she could see right through her. "He's a handsome cuss. And single, same as you. Maybe you ought to try thinkin' of somethin' to say to 'im."

"I'd rather not."

"Could be you could get a little romance goin'."

"I'm not in the market for a romance. If I was, I might go after one of those six handsome cuss, single sons of yours," Kate countered, teasing the gruff older woman.

"Which one would you like? I'm tryin' my best to get 'em married off but they're too mule-headed for their own good."

Kate laughed in spite of having her bluff called. "I don't want one of your sons, either, Junebug. I'm not interested in fooling with any man right now."

"Should be."

"Well I'm not. And Matt's as bad as you are about Brady—he's trying to throw me together with him by hook or by crook. So do me a favor and put me to work in here."

Junebug looked her up and down, as if debating about granting Kate's wish.

Then she went to the swinging door that connected the dining room and said, "Would somebody get Kate outta my kitchen so's I can do some dishin' out of this food without her underfoot?"

"Thanks," Kate said under her breath.

Junebug grinned. "Two by two—that's how we're meant to walk this earth."

Kate just rolled her eyes at the woman as demands for her to go into the dining room were voiced in answer to Junebug's request.

So, with no other choice, that was what Kate had to do.

Rather than serving appetizers buffet-style Junebug had had everyone take their seats at the dining table. But the only place setting that wasn't already occupied when Kate joined her family was the one directly across from Brady.

She would have preferred being situated farther away from him and without much of a view of the houseguest, but as it was she had to take the sole remaining spot.

The McDermot family was once more laughing at something Brady had said as they passed hors d'oeuvres of bruschetta, cherry peppers stuffed with proscuitto and cream cheese, and blue-cheese torta served on crackers. Kate didn't attempt to join in the fun but merely slipped into her seat, wondering as she did if she'd been manipulated once more by Matt, or if all her brothers, sisters-in-law and Matt's fiancée were conspiring against her.

"Brady's been in Alaska since we saw him in Vegas," Matt updated Kate then.

"Ah," she said, unsure what else she was suppose to contribute to that.

But Shane saved her the trouble by asking if Brady had done any hunting or fishing while he was there.

As Brady talked about his adventures, Kate couldn't help checking him out.

He'd obviously taken that shower he'd been headed for. He looked refreshed, and she could smell the spicy scent of cologne or soap or whatever it was he'd used. She only wished she didn't like it so much.

He had changed into a less-worn pair of jeans and a crisp white dress shirt with the sleeves rolled to midforearms and the top button unfastened. It wasn't unusual attire by any means, but what those slight exposures let her see made her all too aware of more details about him than she wanted to be aware of. His thick, straight neck, for instance, and the wholly masculine hollow of his throat. Powerful-looking forearms and wrists that were unaccountably sexy. Not to mention big, blunt-fingered, capable hands.

He'd washed his hair, too, and recombed it, along with shaving away the shadow of a day's growth of beard so that his raffishly handsome face was free of anything that could hide its glory. And even the way his razor-sharp jaw flexed when he chewed somehow tweaked a sensual nerve inside her.

Why hadn't Junebug let her stay in the kitchen? Kate lamented to herself as she fought not to look at Brady, not to be so impressed by him.

But there she was, with nowhere to run and a mysterious disability that left her unable not to study his every movement, unable not to hang on his every word as he told stories about Alaskan winter days when light only dawned for a few brief minutes.

Alaskan winter days that left Kate thinking about endless hours of darkness that someone else might have shared with him....

She was grateful when Junebug finally served dinner and allowed her a distraction from that thought. And the odd bit of something that felt like jealousy that came with it.

The older woman had made Caesar salad, a crown rib roast, braised potatoes and carrots and home-baked rolls. Ordinarily Junebug either prepared dinner in advance and left it to be reheated when the McDermots were ready to eat, or left the cooking for someone else to do so she could go home to her own family. But on special occasions she catered and served the whole meal.

Tonight was one of those nights. So not until all the food was on the table did she inform them that dessert was ready and waiting in the kitchen whenever they wanted it and that she was leaving them to their own devices.

As everyone bade her a nice evening and dug into her delicious fare, Matt said, "I have it set up for you to take a look at those three spreads tomorrow, Brady. Ted Barton's ranch next door is probably the best of the lot but he hasn't made a firm decision to sell yet. The other two have been on the market for a couple of months. The houses on them aren't in as good shape as the Barton place. 'Course I know you care more about the land and the barn than where you'll be livin', but still."

Kate stopped cold and paid closer attention to what was being said as her other brothers chimed in with information on land that was for sale around Elk Creek.

Was she understanding this correctly? Was Brady buying property? *Here?* Was he *moving* here?

It was news to Kate. And not good news. She'd thought that after getting through this visit he would go back to Oklahoma. It had never occurred to her that he might be in Elk Creek permanently.

Suddenly she could feel the blood drain from her face and a cold clamminess settle over her.

"You want to buy a ranch *here?*" she heard herself blurt out with no small amount of alarm.

For the first time since she'd sat at the table, Brady

leveled blue-gray eyes on her. ''Thinkin' about it,'' he answered simply enough.

Her brothers continued filling him in on the pros and cons of each property and what might or might not be factors in the sale prices as they all ate. But Kate couldn't seem to swallow so much as a morsel of food from that moment on. She just kept thinking, He could be here to stay. He could be here to stay....

Most of the rest of the evening was pretty much a blur to her after that. She pushed the food around her plate and pretended to be interested in what was being said at the table. She even managed a remark or two when she'd been silent for longer than she should have been.

But the truth was, she heard almost nothing as the idea of Brady ending up as her next-door neighbor tormented her.

And when she could finally excuse herself without raising eyebrows, she stood to do just that.

Only, before she actually got to say her goodnights, Matt said, ''By the way, Kate, we're all tied up tomorrow, so I thought maybe you could show Brady those properties he needs to see.''

''Me?'' Kate said, the alarm again in her tone.

''You know your way around well enough now. None of the places are hard to find. It'll give you somethin' to do.''

''Who says I need something to do?'' Kate said lamely and much too quickly, sounding like a put-upon younger sister who didn't appreciate her big brother taking liberties with her time.

"What do you have to do?" Matt challenged.

For the life of her, Kate couldn't think of anything except that she wanted to strangle her brother.

Then Brady piped up. "It's all right. Just draw me a map. I'm sure I can find the places myself."

It was clear that Brady had noticed she didn't want to play tour guide, and Kate not only knew she was being rude again, but she could feel the tension in the room because of it.

Yet Matt still wouldn't let her off the hook. "Kate doesn't have anything planned she can't rearrange. Do you?"

All eyes were on her, and she knew her next words would set the tone for the rest of Brady's visit. If she refused, everyone would be aware of just how much she didn't want to be around him. They would all want to know why—especially since she and Brady had seemed to hit it off so well in Las Vegas. And her entire family would be embarrassed by her behavior and feel awkward whenever everyone was together.

But if she didn't refuse she was going to end up spending the whole next day with Brady. Alone with Brady. And all the unsettling things merely being around him did to her.

Maybe strangling Matt wasn't harsh enough punishment.

Kate took a breath and opted for keeping the peace and maintaining appearances. "Sure I can rearrange things. No problem. I'd be happy to show you around," she said without enthusiasm.

"Great," Brady answered much the same way.

With nothing more to be said, Kate finally told everyone good-night and went to her rooms, thinking of ways to get even with her brother as she did.

That was still what she was thinking about an hour later when a soft tap sounded on her door.

"If this is you, Matt, you're dead meat," she muttered to herself.

She'd undressed by then, and before answering the knock she pulled on a navy-blue velvet robe over the supersize T-shirt she was wearing to bed. But she didn't fasten it, because she assumed her late-night visitor was her brother and he'd seen her in her sleep-wear innumerable times before. He'd probably come to gloat about his victory or chastise her for not being more warm and friendly to Brady, she thought, letting the robe hang open to her ankles and padding in bare feet to fling open her door.

But it wasn't Matt standing in the hall outside. Or any of her other brothers, either. It was Brady.

"Oh!" she exclaimed, fumbling instantly with the open sides of her bathrobe to pull them around her.

But not before Brady's gaze dropped enough to take in the Wyoming Women are Wild, Wicked and Willing printed across the front of her shirt—a gag Christmas gift from Matt that caused just the corners of Brady's mouth to tilt upward.

Kate yanked the tie belt around her waist and tied it to make sure she was wrapped up good and tight.

"I'm sorry to bother you," Brady said in a hushed voice, obviously to keep his impromptu visit clandestine. He raised his chin, pointing in the direction of the room behind her. "Can I come in?"

She wanted to say no and avoid more of what it was doing to her to merely think about having him in her rooms, alone, this late at night, wearing nothing but a T-shirt and a bathrobe.

But he had a manila envelope in one hand and enough of an air of formality about him to let her know he was only there on business.

Business she needed to attend to.

So Kate stepped back and motioned him into the sitting room.

He didn't hesitate to come in, but he did take a quick glance up and down the hall a split second before. And he made sure to close the door behind him as soon as he could. Very quietly.

That spicy scent that had caught her attention at dinner wafted in after him, and Kate had the urge to close her eyes and take a few deep breaths. But she resisted. She also tried not to notice how Brady seemed to fill the room just by his presence in it, tried not to feel the warm rush of something that seemed dangerously like excitement.

But trying and succeeding were two different things.

Brady held up the manila envelope. "Divorce papers. As promised," he said, as if he'd brought a treasure map they'd both been searching for.

It didn't feel good to her, though, and Kate didn't know why.

"I wanted to go over them with you," he continued. "To make sure you know what's in them. Not that they're complicated, but just to make sure we're clear on everything."

"Okay," she said, hearing the clipped tone of her voice and resolving to amend it. The divorce had been at her insistence, she reminded herself. It was what she wanted. It was the logical thing to do.

And the baby? a little voice in the back of her mind asked.

But she didn't know yet how she was going to handle letting Brady know about the baby, and she certainly wasn't inclined to blurt out the news to him right then.

"Why don't you sit down?" she invited primly, nodding toward the sofa, two overstuffed chairs and the coffee table that were positioned to face the fireplace and the French doors on the outside wall.

"Thanks."

He crossed the room in long strides of massive legs she had no doubt could control a stallion with nothing but their pressure.

But the fact that he went ahead of her to the couch left Kate with a view of his backside, too. A view she couldn't resist taking in. A view of broad shoulders and a straight back that narrowed to his waist and to a rear end that made her mouth go dry.

She might have been a virgin until two months ago but that didn't mean she hadn't done her fair share of looking at men's physiques—especially their derrieres. And Brady's was the best she'd ever seen.

Only when he sat down and deprived her of the

sight did she realize she'd been ogling him and cut it short to follow him to the sitting area of the room.

He was at one end of the sofa, so she sat in the chair that was at a forty-five-degree angle to it, grateful that she wouldn't have to sit beside him to see the papers he was setting out on the coffee table. But even from there she caught a whiff of the clean, spicy scent of him, and it went right to her head.

Maybe it was the pregnancy, she told herself. She'd noticed that her sense of smell was heightened, so maybe it wasn't so much that he *really* smelled wonderful, but that she merely had some kind of illusion that he did.

Except that it didn't seem like an illusion. It seemed as if he just plain smelled terrific.

"This is pretty straightforward," he said then, flipping through the pages as he spoke. "A simple dissolution of marriage. Basically what's on all these pages amounts to declarations that we have no joint property or assets to split up, no mutual residence for one of us to keep and the other to move out of, no children so no custody or visitation issues."

Kate's mouth went dry, and she didn't hear the rest of what he was saying.

No children so no custody or visitation issues...

Somehow it hadn't occurred to her that the baby she was carrying should be included in the divorce papers. Custody and visitation? Those were things she hadn't even thought about.

Of course, she hadn't really thought about much of anything in terms of Brady and the baby. She hadn't had time to think about it. In the four days since she'd had her pregnancy confirmed, she hadn't thought about much of anything except the fact that she actually was pregnant.

It had come as such a shock. The first period she'd missed hadn't even made her curious. Her cycles had always been irregular and it wasn't unusual for her to skip a period, so she hadn't thought a thing about it. It was only when she realized she'd missed a second one that she'd put two and two together.

And in those four days since she'd taken the home pregnancy test and then gone in to see a doctor in Cheyenne to have it verified, she'd mainly been walking around in a daze. About the only thing she'd actually thought through was that she wanted the baby. But beyond that, well, she was still just trying to come to grips with everything.

"Don't sign anything," Brady was saying, the first words to penetrate her thoughts since child custody and visitation. But "Don't sign anything" seemed to come as a reprieve, so maybe that's why it got through to her.

"Read it all when you have a chance," he advised, "that way you'll know what's there. Then it has to be signed in front of a notary. When we've done that, I'll send it back to the lawyer and he'll file it with the courts."

"A notary," Kate repeated to prove she was listening and to cover up that she hadn't been before.

"It's all just a formality, but we have to do it right for it to be legal."

"But Elk Creek is a small town. If we get a notary here word is bound to leak, and this won't be only between you and me anymore."

"We'll work something out. Maybe we'll trump up an excuse to fly into the nearest town and do it there in a day or so."

That seemed like a reasonable solution. And with Matt in matchmaker mode, her brother would likely not question any time she and Brady shared.

"And that's about it," Brady concluded, tapping the edges of the pages on the coffee table to make sure they were all even before he laid them on top of the envelope. "I'm sorry it took so long for me to get here with this. But my buddy in Alaska had an accident that put him in the hospital, and if I hadn't gone up there and flown for him until he was back on his feet, he would have lost his charter company."

"It's okay," Kate assured. "I thought it would take some time."

The mention of Alaska brought a return of that strange twinge of jealousy she'd felt earlier. And that strange twinge of jealousy compelled her to say, "So Alaska, huh? You talked at dinner about all you did there, but I imagine you met a lot of interesting people, too."

"Sure. I met a lot of interesting people. It's an interesting place."

"Anyone...special?"

She didn't have the courage to look straight at him when she asked that, so she pretended to restraighten the divorce document before slipping it back into the manila envelope. But out of the corner of her eye she saw Brady smile for the first time since he'd come into the room. A small smile, but a smile she remembered well from Las Vegas. A smile that made a warm rush of something she couldn't pinpoint run through her.

Unless of course the smile was due to a happy thought about another woman....

"Did I meet anyone special?" he repeated.

"You know, like did you run into Eskimos or fur trappers or bear hunters?" she persisted.

"I met a few of all those."

"But not many women, I imagine. I read not long ago that there's still a low ratio of women to men. Is that true?"

"Are you askin' if we should add adultery as grounds for the divorce?" he joked.

"No," she said as if the very thought were outlandish.

"Well, you can relax. I was too busy for romance, and what you read is right, I didn't run into many women. Especially not many available ones. The irreconcilable differences as grounds for the divorce will have to stand."

"That doesn't matter to me. I was really only curious about Alaska's population," she fibbed. Badly.

"Either way."

Despite the fact that he seemed to have seen through her, the news that he hadn't hooked up with another woman in the past two months brightened

Kate's spirits considerably. Although she didn't want to think about why it should.

Then he changed the subject. "Seems like you've managed to keep the whole marriage thing under wraps."

"Nobody knows anything," she confirmed. *And you don't know all you think you do.*

"That's good. Then we'll be able to take care of it without anyone being the wiser."

Oh, if only that were true for the long run....

"And what about you? Are you still mad at me?" he ventured carefully, as if he were afraid he might set off the same reaction he had on New Year's morning.

Kate was embarrassed at the memory of her behavior and decided this was the opportunity she needed to apologize for it. "I know I went a little wacko the next morning. It's just that doing what we did... Well, it was so out of character for me. I'm such a straight arrow...." She wished this were coming out more smoothly, but the awkwardness of the situation was making for a bumpy road. "Anyway, I want you to know that in spite of what I said then, I accept that I'm just as responsible as you are for this whole thing."

"So I'm not the devil incarnate anymore?" Brady asked with a note of wry levity to his voice.

"No. I was out of line that next morning. My memory of New Year's Eve isn't clear but it's clear enough to know that no one twisted my arm. I was all for getting married. And the rest,'' she added under her breath.

Brady's smile stretched into a grin. ''Why am I gettin' the impression that you're blamin' yourself now?''

Maybe because she was. Or at least she had been for the past four days, ever since finding out she was pregnant.

Which also happened to be about the same time she'd begun hearing her mother's voice in her head.

Her mother's voice from her growing-up years when her mother had done a lot of preaching about the girl in any girl-boy relationship being the guardian of the gate.

It wasn't something Kate had thought about in years. But suddenly there it had all been again.

The guardian of the gate.

The guardian of the gate, who wouldn't be in this pickle if only she'd maintained some control, some moderation in the amount of champagne she'd consumed on New Year's Eve. If she hadn't given in to her own baser needs, no matter how strong they'd been. If she'd resisted the temptation of sweet, seductive words, the temptation of the handsome cowboy. If she hadn't allowed herself to be swept away by the desires he'd raised in her....

Maybe Brady read the answer to his question in her expression, because when she didn't say anything he said, ''Things are pretty foggy in my memory, too, but as I recall, getting married was my idea. You just thought it was a good one and went along with it. I think that makes the blame pretty much equal.''

Kate shrugged, still feeling at fault no matter what he said. But what was the use in arguing about it? ''I just wanted you to know I don't bear you the kind of ill will I did that next morning.''

Brady chuckled—a deep, rich sound that rolled from his throat. ''That was definitely ill will all right. I was grateful there were no knives in the room or you might have gelded me. You made it clear you thought I was a big bad beast.''

Kate flinched at the reminder. And the truth in it. ''I'm sorry. I was out of line. It isn't what I think of you now.'' What she thought of him now was that he was too good-looking and charming and charismatic and sexy for her own good.

''But you still weren't too happy to see me today,'' he said, sounding as if he doubted her claim.

''Were you happy to see me?'' she challenged in return.

He didn't answer right away. Instead he stared at her with eyes so intense she could almost feel his gaze. So intense she finally had to look directly at him, too, to see if she could read what he was thinking.

But before she could he let out another of those wry chuckles and said, ''I didn't expect to be happy to see you, no.''

Did that mean he had been? Because that's what it sounded like. And the possibility that he'd been happy to see her made something inside her dance.

Then he looked away, as if he didn't want her to see what was in his expression. And he changed the subject once more. "Don't feel like you have to go through with showing me around tomorrow. I know Matt railroaded you. He seems to have his matchmaking hat on again. Or is it *still?*"

"You don't want me to show you around?"

"No, it isn't that," he said quickly. "I had a good time checking out Vegas with you. It'd be nice to learn about Elk Creek the same way. It's just that if you'd rather not—"

"No, it's okay," she heard herself say for no reason she understood. Here he was, giving her a break, and rather than take it, she was getting herself in deeper by making it seem as if she *wanted* to be his tour guide.

Maybe it was because memories of what a good time she'd had with him in Nevada had sprung to mind and made the prospect of repeating it appealing to her. So appealing that she'd forgotten for a moment that she was supposed to be steering clear of him.

"You're sure?" he asked.

Too late now even if she wasn't.

So, trying to cover her tracks, she said, "Matt will never let up if he doesn't think he's getting his way."

"Matt," he muttered, as if he'd thought her reasons had been her own. And for a split second he looked disappointed.

But then he seemed to rebound. "You think we

should play along with his matchmaking, just to keep him off our backs?''

"It might be our only chance." *Oh, you fraud, you,* a little voice in the back of her mind chastised, when a part of her knew full well that she wasn't merely agreeing to spend time with Brady to appease her brother.

"We'd only be pretending, of course," she said. "And there wouldn't be anything to it but things like letting ourselves be thrown together once or twice. We talked about being friends, and that would really be all we were doing. It's just that Matt wouldn't know it."

"Only pretending," Brady repeated.

But there seemed to be some reservation in his tone, and Kate wasn't sure why.

"Unless you don't want to," she said, reversing course in case he was having second thoughts. "I mean, if you want to just hang out with Matt, we can sit him down and tell him point-blank that what he wants to happen is not going to happen, no matter what he does."

"You think that would help?"

Kate hated that he sounded so hopeful.

"It might."

"Or it might not," Brady pointed out. "But if we go along with a few of his maneuverings—"

"And then tell him we're just going to be friends after that, we'll have something to back it up. We can say we tried but we just didn't click."

"Sounds like a plan," Brady agreed. "And it'll

be the perfect cover for getting to a notary with these papers, too.''

"True.''

"So, tomorrow. Matt wants to give me the tour of this place in the morning. Why don't we shoot for leaving around one in the afternoon? After lunch?''

"Fine.''

Had they really just talked themselves into spending part of Brady's visit to Matt with each other instead?

They had. And Kate couldn't believe she'd let it happen. Hadn't she spent nearly every minute since she'd found out Brady was coming thinking of ways to stay away from him?

What had gotten into her?

But Brady stood just then, and she stood with him, hoping that if he left, she could get a handle on what she'd just done.

He didn't leave, though. Instead he was studying her again, as if he wanted to relearn her face.

"You really do look good,'' he said after a moment.

"You, too.'' She'd meant that to be a simple volley, but it had come out much more seriously, much more heartfelt, and she had the sense that she'd just exposed something she shouldn't have.

"Tomorrow then,'' she reminded, hoping he'd take the hint before she gave away anything else.

He didn't respond, though. He just continued staring at her, looking into her eyes now in the same way he had just before he'd kissed her for the first time in Las Vegas.

Was he going to kiss her?

Alarms went off in her mind that told her to move away. To shove him toward the door, if she had to, to get him out of there.

But that wasn't what she did.

Instead she stayed rooted to the spot, gazing up into those eyes that were the color of a summer sky before a storm, her chin tilted, thinking about the way his lips had felt against hers New Year's Eve—sweet and gentle and oh, so adept....

But a kiss didn't come.

All of a sudden he broke the hold he'd seemed to have over her and repeated, "Tomorrow. Afternoon. To keep Matt happy." Then he headed for the door.

Kate didn't follow. She couldn't have, even if she'd wanted to, because thinking about him kissing her and then not being kissed had somehow left her drained. As if dashed anticipation had sapped her strength.

Brady opened the door, peered out to make sure the coast was clear and then said, "'Night."

"Good night," she answered, watching him step out into the hall.

Only after the door closed softly behind him did Kate feel as if she were breathing freely once more. But as she found the strength to go into her bedroom, it occurred to her all over again that she'd just agreed to precisely what she shouldn't have agreed to—spending time with Brady.

What was there about the man that always had her doing the wrong thing? Even when she knew just how wrong it was? How much of a mistake it was? What was it about him that attracted her to him even when she didn't want to be? That had her thinking about kissing him even when she wanted him to leave her alone?

She didn't understand it. Not any of it. But then, there were a lot of things she didn't understand about herself and her actions since meeting Brady. In fact, she'd been more confused than she'd ever been in her life.

Maybe she'd had some kind of breakdown over Dwight and just hadn't known it, she thought, as she got into bed and pulled the covers up to her chin. And then she'd met Brady right after that, and maybe meeting someone in the middle of a breakdown caused a person to do bizarre, out-of-character things. And to go on doing bizarre, out-of-character things.

But she didn't actually think a person could have a breakdown and not know it.

Which left her back where she'd started—with no explanation for why she'd done the things she'd done with Brady on New Year's Eve or why she was doing the things she was doing now.

Right now.

Because even as she hashed through it all in her mind, at that moment there was still a part of her that was actually disappointed he hadn't kissed her.

And if that wasn't confusing, nothing was.

Chapter Four

One of the good things about knowing she was pregnant—if you could call it a good thing—was that Kate finally knew why she'd been waking up nauseous every morning. Without revealing her condition, she'd done some subtle, conversational questioning of Shane's wife, Maya—who had found out she was pregnant at Christmastime—and garnered some help for it. Maya had said she'd had morning sickness early on, and to counteract it she'd kept soda crackers on her nightstand to eat before she'd even raised her head from the pillow each morning.

So that was what Kate had started doing—sneaking soda crackers into her room at night to nibble the minute she woke up.

The next morning, as she lay in bed doing that her

thoughts trailed back to the previous evening. To Brady. And to what to do about him in conjunction with this baby that was making her feel so bad at that moment.

Should she tell Brady she was pregnant now, before the divorce went through? she asked herself. Or later? Or at all?

She really hadn't had time yet to think about whether or not to tell him, but Brady's offhand mention of custody and visitation had made her realize she had to at least consider what she was going to do.

It was tempting not to tell him at all. Ever. To just keep the baby to herself. To have it be her baby and her baby alone.

But in spite of the temptation, she knew that wouldn't be the right thing to do. The baby wasn't hers alone, and she knew Brady had a right to know about it.

But when? Sooner rather than later seemed to be the answer to that. At least it was the answer since he might be moving to Elk Creek. If he ended up living nearby, eventually he would notice. And count back. And know. And she didn't want him finding out that way. That was the coward's way.

But that still didn't mean she had to tell him immediately. Immediately being before the divorce was final.

And waiting until it was final appealed to her. With good reason.

It hadn't been easy for Kate to grow up with four

brothers. And not just in terms of bumps and bruises, practical jokes and teasing and horseplay that overlooked the fact that she was a girl at all. Growing up surrounded by men had also given her an insider's view into some other aspects of that gender. Goodlooking men had plenty of wild oats to sow and just as many women willing to have a part in sowing them.

She learned how men talked—and thought—about some women and some situations with women. Also, regardless of the fact that they might enjoy the favors of a woman who got drunk and spent the night with them, men didn't think highly of her the morning after.

And if that woman got pregnant? Then they considered the man trapped.

Trapped…

That wasn't only a concept she'd garnered from her brothers, though. She had proof. Kelly McGill— her best friend since kindergarten.

Kelly had gotten together with a friend of Matt's when they were all in high school—Buster Malloy. Kelly and Buster had been madly in love. Inseparable. They'd even been voted the couple most likely to grow old together, and they'd assured everyone that was true.

Then Kelly had gotten pregnant and everything had come apart, even though a quickie marriage followed Kelly's graduation and the end of Buster's first and only year of college.

Maybe the baby wasn't even his, Kate had heard

him say to Matt one afternoon when they hadn't known she was in the next room. Matt had discouraged that idea, reminding Buster that Kelly hadn't so much as looked at anyone else.

"Then I'm trapped, is that what you're saying?" Buster had demanded, sounding furious.

Trapped—the same thing Kate's brothers had said about other guys in Buster's predicament. The same thing she'd heard them talking about after Matt's conversation with Buster, agreeing that, yes, Buster was trapped. Stuck. That he had no way out....

The cracker Kate was slowly munching wasn't helping as much as usual because suddenly she felt her bile rise in spite of it.

Or maybe it was what was going through her mind that was churning her stomach. Because she had no doubt that Brady felt the same as her brothers did about things like an inebriated woman he hardly knew spending the night with him.

And getting pregnant.

He would feel trapped. Stuck. And nothing good could come of that. Nothing good had come of it for Kelly, that was for sure.

Kate knew all her friend had gone through since her shotgun wedding to Buster, because Kate had been right there to hold Kelly's hand through the worst of it. Like right after Buster's frequent rants at Kelly for ruining his life. Like when Buster had shirked his responsibilities to Kelly and the twins she'd delivered six months after their wedding and Kate had needed to pay Kelly's rent so she and the

twins wouldn't be evicted because Buster had disappeared with their rent money. Like when Buster
had announced that he wanted out—that was how
he'd put it, as if he were demanding his release from
the cage of his marriage to Kelly.

Kate had been there to hold her friend's hand then,
too, when Kelly and Buster's relationship had become one battle after another over everything. Poor
Kelly had been left not only with two boys to raise
and support on her own, but with a broken heart and
a whole lot of questions about how Buster could have
stopped loving her so suddenly, so completely. How
he could have turned into someone Kelly didn't even
recognize. How he could have come to hate her.

But the answer had always been the same—Buster
had come to all of that because he'd felt forced to
marry Kelly since he'd gotten her pregnant. He'd felt
trapped and stuck.

And if it wasn't enough for Kate to have seen with
her own eyes how bad a situation the unplanned
pregnancy had put her friend in, she'd had Kelly on
the phone the night before her doctor's appointment
reminding her how bad things still were, even ten
years later.

Kate fought another overwhelming spell of nausea,
wishing even as she did that Kelly hadn't been leaving for a vacation in Mexico the same day Kate had
gone to the doctor in Cheyenne. Kate had told her
friend she was afraid she might be pregnant but now
that she knew for sure, now that she was facing
Brady, she craved Kelly's support.

Not that she couldn't guess what her friend would tell her if she could talk to her, Kate thought.

Kelly would say to let the divorce go through before Kate told Brady anything. Kelly would say that just learning about the baby would likely make Brady feel some sort of obligation, but at least if he was already off the hook in the marriage department Kate could make it clear that she didn't need anything from him. That besides being part owner of the ranch she was also opening an accounting and bookkeeping service in town and would make an adequate living at that, so she could afford to support both herself and the child. And, while raising a child alone was a daunting proposition, millions of women did it and she could, too. Kelly was, after all.

"But if I tell him before the divorce is final, he won't believe I mean it," Kate said out loud, as if she were actually talking to Kelly. He would believe she didn't want the divorce at all. That she wanted him to stay married to her.

And he'd most definitely feel trapped.

But Kate was bound and determined that Brady Brown was not going to feel—or be—trapped by her.

No man was going to be married to her because he *had* to be. No man was going to accuse her of the things Buster had accused Kelly of. No man was going to blame her for ruining his life.

The cracker hadn't worked at all and Kate flung the covers aside and made a mad dash to the bathroom where she spent the next twenty minutes being miserable.

When the bout was finally over, she went to the sink, splashed cool water on her face and brushed her teeth.

Being alone in all this was definitely not something she would have chosen for herself. In fact, recalling what Maya had told her about Shane made Kate feel a little jealous. Apparently her brother had waited outside the bathroom door for his wife every time she'd gotten sick, ushered her back to bed and served her fresh crackers when she'd thought she could tolerate them again.

That would be nice. Much nicer than the way things were for Kate—having to suffer through the illness alone, all the while hoping no one realized she was ill at all and why.

And if the person keeping her company, taking care of her, could be Brady?

She chased that notion away, knowing it was dangerous to even entertain such a fantasy. Because in reality, if he knew and if he were there by her side for this, it wouldn't be because he wanted to be, the way Shane had, but because he felt he had to be, the way Buster had. And he would resent her the way Buster had. He'd resent her the way Buster resented Kelly. He would resent the baby the way Buster resented his twins. He'd resent being trapped....

Kate took a few deep breaths in an attempt to fight off another wave of nausea, feeling more convinced by the minute that thinking about Brady this morning was making her more ill than usual.

Or at least the tension of thinking about letting him

know about the pregnancy certainly wasn't helping matters. Any more than actually telling him was likely to.

So, no, she was not going to tell him right away. Definitely not before the divorce was over and done with and he was a free man again.

Then, when he knew without a doubt that she wasn't angling for anything from him, when he had proof that she wasn't interested in trapping him into being married to her, then she'd tell him.

The deep breaths—or maybe having come to a decision and found a semblance of a plan—helped stave off another bout of sickness, and Kate was left standing at the sink, staring at herself in the mirror above it.

Not a pretty sight, she knew. Certainly not a sight for a man who didn't love her. Who probably wouldn't even like her if he felt forced to be with her.

So could she pull off keeping this a secret until the time was right? she asked herself.

Looking for an answer, her gaze dropped from her messed-up hair and almost-gray face to check for other signs of what was going on in her body, to be sure there was nothing overt enough to give her away before she was ready for Brady to know.

She pulled down on the T-shirt she'd worn to bed, making it flatten against her, and turned to look at her profile.

Her breasts were bigger, fuller. But that was only an improvement, since she was not normally busty.

And there was only the tiniest pooch in her ordinarily flat stomach, which the doctor had told her wasn't really more than the hormones relaxing her muscles in preparation for stretching to accommodate the growth that would take place.

It was still a pooch, though.

She stood up straighter, pulled her shoulders back and let go of the T-shirt to see what happened if she practiced good posture and wasn't molding the shirt to her abdomen.

Invisible, she decided, reassuring herself that no one would notice anything.

Which was good. Because that way she could keep her secret as long as she needed to. Long enough for the divorce papers to be filed and for her to pick and choose when she'd let the world know she was going to be a single mother. A single mother who didn't need any man, let alone one who wasn't with her solely because he wanted to be.

And if, deep down, she recognized a little part of her that wished Brady *did* want to be with her through this?

That was probably just a remnant of Dwight's damage, she told herself. The damage that had left her self-esteem battered, that had left her craving a man like Brady, who found her attractive and desirable. The damage that had gotten her into this mess in the first place.

It didn't have anything to do with Brady himself.

Or his eyes that seemed to sear through her.

Or his big, callused hands she barely remembered the feel of.

Or the lips she'd wanted much too much to kiss last night....

But those weren't thoughts she would let herself have.

Because for one brief period of time she might have sacrificed her dignity to the passion that those eyes and hands and lips had evoked in her.

But that time had passed.

And she'd lost all the dignity she ever intended to lose.

Even if he did smell like heaven and have the power to melt her insides with a smile.

Luckily Kate's date with Brady wasn't until one o'clock that afternoon, because it took nearly until noon for the morning sickness to subside. When it finally did, she showered and dressed in an oversize camel-colored turtleneck sweater and a pair of black slacks.

She swept her curly hair up to her crown and held it there with a halo of tiny butterfly-shaped clips, applied just enough blush to hide the pallor of her skin and a little mascara to darken her eyelashes.

Then she gave herself a firm talking-to about keeping her perspective with Brady, and went out to the kitchen where everyone who was home today was gathered for lunch.

Lunch was a more casual affair than dinner. Brady, Buzz, Ry, Shane, Matt and little Andrew sat around the U-shaped breakfast nook. The men were talking horses, and Andrew was playing with a plastic replica of one while Junebug piled their plates with chili, thick hoagies, potato salad, pickles, olives and carrot sticks no one was touching. Maya, Tallie and Jenn sat on bar stools around the counter island at the opposite end of the kitchen, dining on lighter fare and discussing Buzz's upcoming eightieth birthday bash when Kate joined them.

She tried to be a part of the discussion but in truth she found it difficult to take her eyes off Brady even from that distance.

She wasn't watching him directly, of course. Only peripherally, except for the few occasions when a burst of male laughter or a comment tossed across the span of the kitchen gave her an excuse to look his way. But still, she was very much aware of every detail.

He'd already been seated in the nook when she'd arrived, but she could still see that he was wearing snakeskin cowboy boots and faded blue jeans under the table. Above the table he sported a navy-blue Western shirt beneath a leather vest that looked like an old friend.

He was clean shaven, and his hair was combed but not so neatly that it appeared as if he'd taken pains with it. Instead it seemed as if he might have tended to it after his own shower and since then had run a hand or two through it.

He looked much like her brothers did—cowboys all, in for the midday meal after half a day's work.

But for some reason to Kate, Brady stood out from the crowd.

Maybe it was his darker coloring, she thought as she gingerly ate half a turkey sandwich and tried to figure out why her gaze kept tracking to him like a heat-seeking missile.

Maybe it was the voice that was only slightly lower than her brothers' but seemed to draw her attention every time he spoke despite the fact that he wasn't talking to her.

Or maybe what made him seem so unique was his laugh. A full, booming, uninhibited laugh filled with gusto and a zest for life.

Or maybe it was just some primitive, elemental connection between the two of them because of the baby that secretly joined them.

Whatever the cause, to Kate he seemed head and shoulders above her brothers in every way. He seemed more striking looking. More animated. More appealing. More charming. More masculine. More of everything potent and powerful and irresistible.

More of everything that clouded her thinking and put all her senses into overdrive.

Which was why she shouldn't be spending the afternoon alone with him. But there was no backing out of it now and she knew it would only be a waste of energy to try.

He's just a guy, she told herself, trying to regain that perspective she'd promised herself on the way out of her rooms. Just a guy like a gazillion other guys her brothers had brought around over the years.

And maybe if she could actually convince herself of that, the next few hours would be okay.

Everyone finished eating shortly after one, and the men slid out of the breakfast nook, ready to get back to work.

Buzz shuffled Andrew out of the kitchen for a nap, Ry and Shane kissed their wives and headed for the barn, and that left Matt and Brady to join everyone else at the island counter.

"Why don't you guys take my truck," Matt said then, aiming the suggestion at both Kate and Brady, and obviously referring to their imminent departure to check out the properties.

"We can use my car," Kate countered in an attempt to maintain as much control as she could—in outward things, even if she wasn't having much success with the inward.

"Brady'll be as uncomfortable in that little go-cart of yours as we all are when we have to ride in it," Matt argued. "I don't need the truck today, so take it." Then, as if that settled it, he pulled a full key ring out of his pocket and held it up like a bone for a dog. "Who's driving?"

Kate snatched the keys before Brady had a chance. "Me. I'm the one who knows where we're going, remember?"

"Not until I tell you, you don't," Matt reminded. But then he went on to explain which ranches were up for sale and how best to get to them.

"You sure you don't mind her drivin'?" Matt asked Brady when he'd finished.

Brady looked at her as if he sensed her need for feeling in command and didn't mind conceding to it. "Nah. No big deal," he answered without taking his blue-gray gaze off Kate.

"You better get goin', then," her brother urged. "You have a lot of ground to cover for one afternoon."

And with that Kate had no choice but to slip off her bar stool and lead the way out to Matt's truck where it was parked in front of the house.

She made sure of one thing, though. She climbed in behind the steering wheel before Brady could open the door for her or give her a hand up or do anything that might put her in closer proximity to him than she needed to be.

He was there to close her door once she'd gotten in, but she only called a curt "Thanks" through the rolled-up window. Then she concentrated on starting the engine, trying not to watch him in the rearview mirror as he rounded the vehicle from behind.

Of course, nothing was aided by his joining her in the cab and bringing with him that spicy scent she liked so well, but what could she do about that? She just tried not to let herself think about it.

"You can drive a rig like this?" Brady asked without preamble, referring to the big pickup truck with dual rear wheels that Matt had bought himself only the month before.

"I grew up on a ranch, remember? I was driving trucks and tractors when I was twelve," she assured him.

He was sitting at an angle, facing her, with one thigh resting sideways on the seat so his ankle could be propped on his other knee. He also had a long arm slung across the top of the seat back, his hand near her nape—something else she didn't want to be so aware of.

As a matter of fact Kate wished he wasn't positioned the way he was at all. It made his attention so directly focused on her that it seemed as if the heat of his eyes was a tangible thing.

But what could she do? She couldn't tell him to face front and stop studying her. At least, she couldn't say that without sounding ridiculous. So instead she just had to add one more thing to the list of what she was working to ignore.

"The Barton place is the closest," she said as she pulled away from the curb and headed for the main road. "Do you want to start there and work our way out, or start at the farthest and work our way back?"

"Let's hit the Bartons' first."

That would have been her choice, just so they wouldn't be in that truck for too long with him sitting the way he was. Maybe when they got in it again he'd sit straight in the seat and quit giving her the once-over.

"Beautiful day," she commented, hoping he might change position to look out at the countryside bathed in warm sunshine. March had definitely come in like a lamb with five consecutive sixty-degree days.

But Brady didn't budge. He just muttered, "Beautiful," without so much as glancing out the window.

Then he said, "Tell me about the Bartons."

Gladly, Kate thought, eager for something to distract her, even if she couldn't seem to distract him.

"Mr. and Mrs. Barton are both nearly seventy," she began. "Their land used to be part of our ranch, but about a year after Buzz bought it he decided he needed an influx of cash for livestock and to build the house, so he sold off several parcels to Ted Barton. My brothers have talked about buying it back if Mr. Barton ever decided to sell. Matt must want you around pretty badly to have talked everybody into letting you have first stab at the place."

"County needs a crop duster," Brady said as if it were the reason Matt had given him.

That was all the time it took to reach the Barton's small white farmhouse, and Kate pulled to a stop in front of it. But as she turned off the engine she continued to tell him about her neighbors. "They have one son who's a stockbroker on Wall Street. He isn't interested in taking over the place but they wish he was, so that's why it isn't formally up for sale. They can't run it anymore, it's more of a drain on them financially than anything else, and the son is urging them to sell. He even has a condominium all ready for them to move into if they'd just do it. But they haven't completely made up their minds. So don't be surprised if they seem a little reluctant."

"Good to know."

Brady got out of the truck and so did Kate, again

in enough of a hurry to preclude him from coming around to open her door. But he didn't go up to the house until she had rounded the pickup and could go ahead of him.

As she did, Kate had the distinct sensation that he was taking a better look at her from behind than at the house he could be buying. She cast a glance back at him to see if she was just imagining things and caught him with his gaze on her rear end.

Knowing he'd been found out, he raised his eyes, but his expression didn't show any contrition. Instead he smiled a lopsided, mischievous smile.

"You're in pretty fine shape today," he said as if his open scrutiny of her had been her own fault for looking the way she did.

Mr. Barton came to the door, apparently having seen them coming. But before Brady acknowledged their host he shot Kate a wicked wink that caused her cheeks to heat. Only then did he turn his attention to the elderly gentleman as Mr. Barton invited them inside.

Kate spent the next hour and a half having tea with Mrs. Barton while Mr. Barton showed Brady around the house and then took him out to the barn. Mrs. Barton was a lovely older woman who kept up a lively chatter, but Kate had trouble following the conversation because her mind—and eyes—kept wandering to Brady whenever he came into sight through the plate glass window beside the kitchen table where the two women sat.

Kate couldn't help asking herself what things

might be like if she and Brady hadn't eloped in Las Vegas. If they'd merely had a good time together on that trip but never taken things that last, disastrous step. She couldn't help asking herself what things might be like if she hadn't gotten pregnant. And if Brady were in Elk Creek merely for a visit and to look at some property now.

Would she have been giving free rein to the attraction she couldn't deny she felt? Would she have been relishing the time with him? Would she have been basking in the chemistry that seemed to be between them?

The answer, she decided, was yes, to everything.

Yes, she might have let the attraction have free rein, because although she didn't know much about him, what she did know led her to believe he was a good, decent, honorable man.

Yes, she probably would have been relishing this time with him because no matter how much she wished it weren't true, she liked being with Brady. Even now, when it was against her will and when she was trying *not* to like being with him. The truth was, she still felt more alive, more energetic and more buoyant just being around him.

And, yes, she would likely have been basking in the chemistry that seemed to be between them, because in her experience that was something hard to find, something to be nurtured and explored when she did encounter it.

But New Year's Eve and ending up pregnant *had* happened, she reminded herself. And because they'd happened, nothing was the way it might have been. Because they'd happened, a simple attraction, a simple pleasure in his company, a not-so-simple chemistry, couldn't run their course, couldn't be indulged in.

And she had to remember that, she told herself sternly. She had to fight against the attraction running any kind of course at all. Because if she didn't fight, if she let things between them go the way they seemed inclined to, she could later be faced with Brady's whole different interpretation of what went on. The way Kelly had been. Like Buster—when Brady *did* learn she was pregnant—he could turn around and say it was all just a ploy she'd been using. A lure. He could say she'd just been pretending things were clicking between them so that when she dropped the bomb of the baby she'd have some emotional leverage.

Besides, to allow things between them to go the way they seemed inclined to was likely to get her in deeper herself. It was likely to get her hurt. The way she'd been hurt by Dwight.

Dwight.

Oh, no, she didn't want to go through that again.

She *wouldn't* go through that again.

And if there had been even the slightest inclination to give in to her attraction to Brady in any way, the memory of Dwight doused it completely and solidified her resolve.

Because no matter what her natural inclination might be, no matter how strong the chemistry between them, it was worth the fight to keep from ever feeling the way she'd felt over Dwight.

Chapter Five

Brady's tour of the other two properties took equally as long as the Barton place had. By the time he was finished for the day, darkness had fallen and he and Kate were on the southernmost outskirts of Elk Creek.

"Looks like we'll be late for supper," Kate observed as they got in the truck to go home. She'd been coming up with inane small talk like that all afternoon for no reason other than to fill time and space with inconsequential noise that helped block out her own thoughts about Brady.

"I was hoping we'd get through early enough for me to take a look at Elk Creek itself," he answered. "Think we could skip supper at the ranch and grab a bite in town so I could still do that?"

And here she'd thought this day was going to end.

Before she could answer, Brady leaned over so that his mouth was nearly at her ear. "I'll make it worth your while and pick up the tab," he said in a seductive voice meant to be a joke.

It worked on both levels, though. It made her smile and proved too alluring for her to resist.

"You only have two choices of restaurants," she warned. "The Dairy King and Margie Wilson's Café—Maya's mother owns that one. The food is good and substantial but nothing fancy."

"Good and substantial will do. But how about we take that drive around town first and eat afterward?"

"Okay."

Since they came into town from the south end they drove past the train station and The Buckin' Bronco honky-tonk owned by Linc Heller, one of Elk Creek's more prominent citizens.

Kate didn't know a whole lot about the people or places that made up the small town, since she'd only been living there a little over two months herself, but what she did know she shared with Brady as they drove down Center Street, the main thoroughfare.

She pointed out the general store, owned by Linc's wife, Kansas, and a number of other shops and businesses all housed in quaint old buildings of one, two and three stories, some brick, some not, but all kept up with obvious care and pride. Then they drove up and down most of the residential streets, too, just so Brady could get the full feel of the place.

"Do you like it here?" he asked when they back-

tracked to the storefront café they'd decided on earlier, with its red-and-white-checkered half curtains in
the twin picture windows that bracketed the entrance
on to Center Street.

"I do," Kate admitted, even though she was
tempted to bad-mouth the small town so he might
think twice about moving there. She wasn't sure why
the idea of that bothered her so much. She told herself she should be glad he'd be in closer proximity
to his child. Close enough to be a part of that child's
life.

But at that moment the only thing she could think
was that it meant more time seeing him from a distance and fighting what that sight did to her.

It was that more-selfish side that won a brief victory when she said, "But if you're not from a small
town and don't know what it's like to live in one
you might be careful. It isn't for everyone. People
who are used to cities aren't always very happy in a
place like Elk Creek."

"I'm not from a small town but I am from a rural
community. I was raised on one of the biggest dairy
farms in an area just outside of Oklahoma City. But
I think I'll do fine here," he concluded, glancing
around the café as if he were surveying his kingdom
and finding it more than acceptable.

Margie Wilson wasn't working tonight, but a teen-
age girl seated them at a table not far from the soda
counter. The restaurant was nearly filled with cus-
tomers, some of whom Kate had met since coming
to town. She exchanged pleasantries and introduced

Brady before taking her seat facing him and the soda counter.

It was the first time she noticed a count-down board hanging on the wall behind it. In large black letters it said Weeks Until Margie's First Grandbaby Arrives, and a hook held a card with the number twenty-two.

The sight of it gave Kate a stab, and again she felt envious of her sister-in-law. Maya's coming baby was anticipated with such delight, while her own was surrounded by drastically different circumstances and had so far brought more fear, worry and turmoil than joy.

Her feelings must have been reflected in her face because Brady said, "You don't like the specials of the day?"

She hadn't even realized the teenager who'd seated them had brought water and recited the specials.

Kate forced herself to focus and said, "I'm sorry. I wasn't paying attention."

As the young girl repeated them, Brady craned around to look behind him at the count-down board that had caused her momentary preoccupation.

When the waitress left them to decide what they wanted, he said, "You did say this place belonged to Maya's mother, didn't you?"

"Margie. Yes."

"But the sign is a surprise to you?"

"No, I was just thinking how nice it is for Maya that her baby is so wanted."

"Why wouldn't it be?"

Kate shrugged. "Some aren't, you know."

"Sure. But Maya and Shane are happily married and a good age for it."

"What about you? Do you want kids?" Kate heard herself ask, when the urge to know became too great and the opening seemed to present itself.

"Someday," Brady answered without hesitation, but also in a way that said it was too far off for him to actually consider it seriously.

"Is that why you're moving to Elk Creek? To settle down?" Kate persisted.

"I suppose it's a beginning of that. It's not as if I have a plan or a time limit or anything like that. I'm movin' to Elk Creek because the farm in Oklahoma really belongs to my brother. He's worked it since our folks passed away, while I've been off flyin' and doin' my own things. I still technically own half of it, but it just doesn't seem like mine anymore. I want a place of my own, even if I have to start small and build up. So I've been workin' my tail off the past few years, savin' everything I could since I paid off the plane, and here I am. But I want a decent house to bring a wife to and a few years alone with her, when I find her, before we bring kids into the mix."

He might not think he had a plan, but it certainly sounded to Kate as though he did. A plan that had nothing to do with her or a baby in seven months. And for some reason she didn't understand, that knocked the wind out of her.

"What about you?" he asked then. "You want kids?"

"Yes," was all she said, in a voice more quiet than she'd intended.

It wrinkled Brady's brow and made him laugh at the same time. "Don't sound so thrilled about it," he said facetiously. "Kids are fun. Look at your nephew. Andrew has more personality than a dozen adults. This morning he had to have coffee with Matt and me—in a coffee mug. We just put a splash in his milk, but he sat there and drank every drop, holdin' the cup the way we were, mimicking everything we were doin'. It was a riot."

Kate nodded. "I know. He loves to play little man," she said, trying to regain her equilibrium.

The waitress came back then, and they ordered. Pot roast and potatoes for Brady, nothing but a bowl of soup for Kate, who had suddenly lost her appetite.

"So tell me about good old Elk Creek," Brady said when the waitress had left.

He was apparently finished with the remote notion of children, and Kate had to concede and change the subject. What else could she do? Especially when she didn't want to alert him prematurely about her pregnancy by showing undue interest in whether or not he wanted to be a father anytime soon. But she was still dispirited and had to put some effort into hiding it when she began to tell him about the small town they'd both chosen to move to.

"The people here are friendly and nice," she said, forcing enthusiasm into her tone. "And neighborly.

Plus there are some fine workmen for hire—carpenters, a plumber and an electrician. I'm opening an accounting office just up the street, and my remodel crew seems to be on the ball and doing a great job. But like I said, it is still a small town. That means everybody knows everybody else's business and there aren't a lot of amenities like a wide variety of restaurants or a shopping mall or things like that.''

She'd finished less upbeat than she'd begun. Not intentionally, but she really was going back and forth on the issue of Brady living in Elk Creek. She just couldn't seem to get ahold of her own roller-coaster emotions where he was concerned.

But he swung the pendulum back toward the positive on his own. ''Elk Creek has some things a lot of other small towns don't have. There's a doctor, a dentist and a school. And Matt says the general store will order in about anything you want even if it isn't normal stock.''

''That's true. And I guess you have the plane to fly in and out whenever you want, so the isolation won't bother you. You'll probably get some charter business, too.''

''The place has a good feel to it,'' Brady said as their meals were served. ''Warm. Welcoming. Laid-back. Some signs of prosperity but no urban sprawl.''

''So you think you'll want to stay,'' Kate concluded.

''You don't sound like you want me to,'' he observed with a slight chuckle.

''No, it isn't that,'' she was quick to say. ''What

I meant was, did you like one of the properties you saw today?''

He didn't look as if she'd fooled him, but he didn't push it. ''Matt was right—the Barton spread is the best of the lot.''

''And Mr. Barton seemed pretty taken with you by the time we left. I think he wanted to adopt you.''

Brady just smiled his acknowledgment of that fact. ''It'd be a good spot for me, too. We could do some co-oping, you McDermots and me. But maybe you wouldn't want me so close by.''

So he did know she was dragging her feet about that.

But she didn't admit it. Instead she said, ''Why? Would you be a bad neighbor?''

''I don't think so. But you might not want to be lookin' at my face that often.''

She looked at it now, studied it in a way she'd been trying to avoid doing all afternoon. His beard was beginning to shadow his cheeks and jaw but she liked the slightly scruffy look it gave him. And those eyes of his, so pale, so gorgeous, could melt her insides with a glance. Not to mention the sharply carved planes of his face, every feature, every angle as perfect as if it had been cut with a confident sculptor's hand.

He was nowhere near hard on the eyes. Which was why it would be so hard on every other part of her to have him within sight whenever she turned around.

"Kate?" he said as if calling to her from a distance.

She realized belatedly that she'd let too much time elapse since he'd wondered aloud if she might be against looking at his face as often as she would have to if he lived next door.

"I'm sure it would be okay," she blurted out, feeling like an idiot. Again.

Brady breathed a wry chuckle. "It took a while to think about, though."

"Well, you know, I don't like to make snap decisions," she joked to cover up.

"Couldn't prove that by me," he returned, teasing her with one raised eyebrow.

"New Year's Eve notwithstanding," she qualified.

"And it helps to ply you with a little champagne."

"A little? Buckets of the stuff is more like what I was plied with *that* night."

His smile was mischievous once more. And oh, so charming. "So if I promise to keep you in a constant supply of champagne, can I buy the Barton place?"

"Will you have it written into the deal as a ransom clause?"

"Maybe just a contingency clause."

"Okay, but I only want the good stuff. No cheap domestic swill for me."

Where was this coming from? she asked herself even as she bantered—and, yes, flirted—with him. Lord, but the man could induce her to behave unlike herself.

Brady was staring at her again. Closely. Intently.

As if he were seeing something he hadn't seen in her before. And liking it.

And she liked that he liked it. Heaven help her....

They'd finished eating by then, and Brady paid the check so they could leave. But before Kate even noticed, he'd grabbed Matt's keys off the table where she'd set them.

"My turn to drive," he announced, standing to pull her chair out—and she hadn't seen that coming, either.

"I don't know if you can handle the truck," she heard herself tease him, still not understanding what had gotten into her. "It's not some puny little airplane, you know," she added as they went out into the cool night air.

"'Puny little airplane'? Watch what you're sayin' about my pride and joy."

He opened the truck's passenger door for her, and while she knew just how dangerous it was, she couldn't help reveling in the feel of his big hand at her elbow, helping her up into the cab. Any more than she could help drinking in the sight of him walking around the front end on long legs that had just a hint of swagger to them.

Then he climbed behind the wheel and adjusted the seat and mirrors, fitting much better there than she had.

He started the engine, turning an ear to it as if to hear it more clearly and said, "She does purr, doesn't she?"

"I beg your pardon. I do not purr." Kate pre-

tended to be offended, knowing perfectly well that
he was talking about the truck and not her.

"Careful, you're talkin' to a man who knows better," he said with a sly sideways glance at her as he
pulled away from the curb.

"Oh, that was low-down and dirty," she said with
a wicked laugh of her own that she didn't know she
even had in her.

He grinned a broad, devilish grin. "But true," he
boasted.

She hit him. A playful smack on the arm, the kind
she'd have given any one of her brothers for teasing
her.

But somehow it didn't feel the same. It sent a
shock wave of awareness of hard, bulging biceps that
reverberated all through her.

"It's good to see you loosen up," Brady said.
"You've been wound tighter than a clock since I got
here."

"Well, it isn't easy for a woman to face her defiler," she said, still joking and unsure where it was
all coming from. Except that it *had* helped her loosen
up and she felt so much better than she had lately
that it wasn't something she wanted to let go of.

"Defiler?" he repeated, sounding shocked but
laughing at the same time.

"Isn't that what you are? A defiler of young virgins?"

"Oh, geez, don't ever say that anywhere near any
of your brothers or I'm a dead man."

"Behave yourself, then, and only do what I tell you to. Or else."

"Blackmail?"

"What can I say? There's an evil side to me."

She had him laughing hard now and she liked it.

Oh, who was she kidding? She liked *him*.

When his laughter had subsided to a chuckle, he glanced at her again. "How did I go without meeting you until Las Vegas?" he asked as if he felt deprived because of it.

"Just lucky, I guess."

"I don't think so," he said more to himself than to her. Then he said, "Seriously. I've been friends with Matt since we were freshmen roommates in college. I'd met all your brothers and your folks before. Where were they hiding you?"

"The cellar. That's where they hide all the virgins in my family."

"Seriously," he insisted on another laugh.

"I was in college, too. I skipped a grade in elementary school, so Matt and I were in the same graduating class. I went off to Denver University when he went to Texas A & M and met you. After that I stayed in Colorado—summers and all. I only went home for the occasional visit. I suppose we were just never visiting at the same time. I'd heard about you, though."

He looked at her from the corner of his eye. "Good things or bad?"

"All bad. What else is there?"

He chuckled again, shaking his head.

They'd arrived home by then, and as Brady turned off the engine he looked at her through eyes so approving she could feel the caress of his gaze. "Well, it was my loss," he said as if he meant it.

He held her mesmerized for a long moment, and Kate had a sudden vivid recollection of being with him in Las Vegas. Of having spent time with him the way they just had, having fun together, teasing, flirting.

And then, as if they were right back there, he reached out a long arm and cupped the back of her head in his hand, pulling her to meet him in the center of the seat so he could kiss her. Only briefly. Just a peck on the lips. But a kiss nevertheless. A kiss with enough impact on her to knock the wind out of her for a second time that night.

But just that quickly it was over, and Brady was out of the truck and coming around to open her door for her. Holding out a hand for her to take to help her out.

Still dazed by his kiss and not thinking clearly, she took his hand, slipping into it as perfectly as if her own had been cut from it, and for the moment he was holding it she savored the feeling of power restrained by gentleness.

But he didn't continue to hold her hand once she was out of the truck and instead let go so they could head for the house without any indication of what had just passed between them.

"I'd better...do some things in my room," she said as soon as they were inside, knowing she needed to distance herself from him before things went any further.

Brady just nodded his acceptance of that and said, "Thanks for today. And tonight. For everything."

"Sure. Thanks for dinner."

He smiled down at her with those thermal blue eyes once more and murmured, "Anytime."

"See you tomorrow."

"G'night," he answered, still studying her.

And oh, how she wanted him to kiss her again! Now, when she was prepared for it and could relish it, rather than be barely aware of anything but the shock and surprise she'd been aware of in the truck.

But he didn't kiss her again.

And she was afraid if she didn't do as she'd said she would and go to her room, she might take the initiative and kiss him herself.

So she muttered an answering good-night and forced herself to turn on her heels and leave him in the entryway.

But she took with her an inordinate urge not to go to her room at all. To go instead past it to his room, to be waiting when he got there.

Of course she didn't do that.

But even after she got to her own room and had closed the door securely behind her, she still imagined that she could taste his kiss on her lips.

And it only tormented her.

Because in spite of everything, she just wanted more.

Chapter Six

"Heads up!" Brady said by way of greeting, when he found Matt alone in the kitchen early the next morning.

Matt raised his head in response, and Brady tossed him the keys to his truck.

"You were behind closed doors when I got in last night," Brady explained. "I thought you would probably rather not be disturbed so I hung on to the keys. Hope you didn't need them before now."

"It's barely seven a.m. Where would I have gone before now?" Matt countered, pouring a second cup of freshly brewed coffee to go with the one already steaming on the counter.

Then Matt picked up both cups and headed for the breakfast nook, nodding to Brady as he did.

Brady accepted the silent invitation and slid into one side of the nook about the same time Matt slipped into the opposite end.

"So how'd it go?" Matt asked after they'd both had a little coffee.

Matt could have been referring to how things had gone in terms of the properties Brady had looked at the day before, or he could have been referring to how things had gone between Brady and Kate, since Matt wasn't making any attempt to hide the fact that he was matchmaking.

Brady opted for assuming his best friend was asking about the properties.

"It went pretty well. You were right about the Barton place being the best of the three. The house needs some work. I don't think the Bartons have painted in fifty years or replaced the carpeting or fixed a shingle or a gutter."

"Yeah but compared to the shacks on the other two spreads, it's a palace."

"True. And there's a great barn plus a good water source. I'm going up to do a fly-by on all three today, get an idea of the terrain of each of them. But I think Bartons' is where I'll make my bid."

"Did he seem agreeable to selling?"

"He didn't sound too reluctant by the time I finished with him yesterday. He said his son had finally convinced him he'd never come back here, so there was no point in their hangin' on to the place. Seems like I should have a pretty fair shot."

"Good."

Matt was participating in the conversation, but Brady could tell he'd chosen the wrong interpretation of his friend's question.

Matt said, "When will you make an offer?"

"Today, maybe. Before the Bartons have too long to think about putting the place formally up for sale and puttin' some competition into the bidding."

"Great. I hope they accept it. Now tell me how it went with Kate."

Brady had to smile at the impression he had of Matt champing at the bit as he waited for an opening to get back to what he'd really wanted to know in the first place.

And Brady just couldn't resist holding out any longer.

"She found the other two spreads without any problem and didn't put any dents in your new truck," he answered, being purposely obtuse.

"And you didn't make it home for supper," Matt persisted. "Which means you stretched yesterday afternoon into the evening."

There was a cue in that for Brady to expound upon. But he wasn't through giving his friend a hard time yet.

"Oh, yeah, I nearly forgot. We stopped off at a justice of the peace between the Bartons' and ranch number two, got married, had triplets between seein' the second place and the third, then got divorced after that because things weren't working out. Irreconcilable differences."

"Funny," Matt said. "How'd things really go with you guys?"

Brady took a deep breath and willed himself to have patience. "What am I gonna tell you, Matt? I think Kate is great. She's beautiful. She's sweet. She's funny. She's fun to be with. But maybe I've lost my touch with women since Claudia, because Kate just isn't interested." Why else would it have taken him so long to break through her defenses just to get her to laugh a little, to joke a little, to lighten up? And between New Year's morning and last night she'd made it damn clear that she didn't want anything to do with him.

"You're wrong," Matt said point-blank.

"She tell you somethin' she's not lettin' me in on?"

"No. And I know she's actin' as if she's not interested. But she is."

"Ah, great Swami, and how do you know this? Tea leaves? A crystal ball? Eerie voices that come to you in the night?"

Matt pointed a finger at one of his own eyes. "I can see it all right. She gets herself spruced up when she knows she'll be crossin' paths with you. She watches you when you're not lookin'. Kinda like you do with her," he added slyly. "Only the two of you just keep pussyfootin' around."

New Year's Eve had not been pussyfooting around. And then there had been last night. Kissing her didn't qualify as pussyfooting around, either. It did, however, count as something he couldn't believe he'd done.

Kissing Kate had been an impulse. A spur-of-the-moment thing. He'd gotten carried away by some inclination, even when he'd been trying like hell *not* to get carried away by his attraction to Kate, because he knew it was a mistake. The same mistake he'd made with Claudia—a mistake he wasn't going to make again. No matter how nice a day he and Kate had had together or how damn good it had felt to kiss her again.

"I think you ought to give this up, Matt," Brady said then, thinking it was advice he needed to take himself. "Kate isn't my biggest fan." Which explained why she'd hardly responded to that kiss last night and then run off the minute they hit the entryway, as if she'd had all she could take of being with him.

"You're wrong," Matt repeated. "She's just shy. Quiet. Inexperienced."

Not as inexperienced as she'd been before New Year's Eve.

But Brady sure as hell couldn't say that!

"You guys just need to get to know each other," Matt continued. "You couldn't have done any of that in Vegas. You were with the whole group of us almost every minute there."

"No, Las Vegas wasn't a good get-to-know-you place, and we hardly did any of that," Brady admitted because it was true. If you didn't count sleeping together. And maybe then what she'd gotten to know about him she hadn't liked. "But still—"

"'But still' nothing. She's watchin' you from under her lashes and you're watchin' her from under yours, and all you need is to stop bein' so wary of each other. Take some time to tell her your stories, to listen to her stories, to find out what you both like and don't like, and you'll see—we could end up more than friends and neighbors."

Yeah, we'll end up ex-brothers-in-law before you know we were ever brothers-in-law to begin with.

"You must've had a little start in that direction yesterday," Matt insisted. "You weren't out past supper time without talkin' to each other. Take your opportunities where you can. Like today, for instance. Kate's plannin' to drive into Cheyenne to do some shopping for Buzz's birthday on Saturday. You'll be taking your plane up, anyway. Why not fly her into the city?"

Brady sighed long and loud. "She's not interested, Matt. And I'm tryin' to avoid what I did with Claudia when *she* wasn't interested."

"Kate is *not* Claudia. Kate is what you deserve. And you're what she deserves after that Dwight jerk."

"Dwight jerk?"

Matt grinned. "I'm not tellin' you about him. Ask her—it's one of her stories."

There just didn't seem to be any getting through to Matt.

"I told you, I've lost my touch with women," Brady said again.

"Well get it back."

Brady rolled his eyes. "Easier said than done."

"Claudia just shocked you. But just because you struck out with her doesn't mean you've lost your touch."

Brady would have liked to believe him. But Kate had disproved it. In a big way. On New Year's morning and again since he'd flown into Elk Creek.

"Take her to Cheyenne today," Matt urged. "Just get to know her. Let her get to know you. Then if it doesn't work out, well, hell, we can still at least be neighbors. I'll fix you up with Jenn's friend Greta when she comes into town for our wedding."

Brady just shook his head, hating that everything Matt said about getting to know Kate only encouraged what he was inclined to do himself. Hating that he *was* inclined that way.

"Come on," Matt coaxed. "You'll thank me in the end."

"Or want to shoot you," Brady said under his breath.

But somehow that didn't sound like the hard line against pursuing Kate that he knew he should be following. Maybe he just never learned.

"I don't know, Matt. I just don't think it's a good idea."

And yet, good idea or bad idea, he knew deep down that he was probably going to do just what his friend was pushing him to do in spite of his show of unwillingness.

Because at the same time Matt was pushing, something else seemed to be pulling him.

And all in the direction of Kate.

Kate was not happy about ending up in Brady's plane. With Brady. Flying to Cheyenne that afternoon.

She'd actually been looking forward to the solitary drive into the city, to a leisurely day of shopping by herself. Especially after all the internal uproar she'd been in since Brady's arrival, topped off by a long, sleepless night of thinking about him and that kiss and what it had done to her. Her afternoon in Cheyenne had seemed like a much-needed reprieve.

But had she gotten that much-needed reprieve? No, she hadn't. Thanks once more to Matt and his machinations and her earlier agreement with Brady to pretend to play along with her brother's attempts at matchmaking.

"The Barton place still looks the best," Brady was saying as he carefully kept an eye on all the dials on the instrument panel as well as the wide blue expanse of a March sky so clear it looked as if milk had been poured into the darkness of night until it was just right.

He went on to talk about the lakes and ponds and sections of the river available to each property—water rights, the ranchman's mantra—but Kate couldn't concentrate on what he was saying. She was too busy reminding herself of all the reasons why she shouldn't be where she was at that moment. All the reasons she shouldn't be noticing how incredibly sexy he was in his black wire-rimmed sunglasses and the worn leather flight jacket that looked so soft it seemed to beg to be touched. All the reasons she shouldn't be so aware of his big hands on the control yoke, deftly keeping the flight steady and smooth.

All the reasons she shouldn't still be thinking about that nothing-of-a-kiss the night before.

But reasons or no reasons, she was noticing and thinking about it all. Along with how good he smelled again. And it was warring inside her with a confusingly heavy heart that made her wonder what was wrong with her.

She knew where the heavy heart was coming from, but knowing its origin and understanding it were two different things. The coup de grâce that had made her agree to this day in Cheyenne with Brady had been when—in the middle of Matt's maneuverings—Brady had leaned over and whispered in her ear that they could have the divorce papers notarized in Cheyenne without any worry of gossip.

From the moment he'd said it she'd known she had to concede to her brother's gambit, but from that very same moment she'd had this heavy heart feeling.

And she definitely couldn't figure out why.

It couldn't be some divorce-related reaction because there was nothing about her that felt married.

But there it was—a reluctance, a sadness, a desire to drag her feet.

Which she certainly couldn't do.

Just because Brady made her blood run faster in her veins whenever he was around didn't mean she should—or could—refuse to finalize the divorce that had been her idea in the first place.

Besides, he really would feel trapped if she showed any hesitancy about signing the papers and then told him she was pregnant to boot.

So she'd said yes to this trip into Cheyenne with him, put the divorce papers in her purse to take along and now had to suffer through World War III going on inside her.

Of course, it also didn't help that Brady seemed so eager to get the divorce done. He apparently really did want out. And the faster the better.

It made her worry about what his response might be to learning she was pregnant.

And it also stung. Which was weird, too. Because it shouldn't have. She should have been able to take it in stride. After all, she didn't want them to stay married. Even above and beyond being determined that Brady not feel trapped, *she* didn't want to stay married to a man she hardly knew. Regardless of the fact that he was the father of her baby. That would be insane and archaic and would no doubt lead to more and more problems, until the inevitable divorce really was traumatic.

But maybe he should *want* to stay married to her,

she thought, knowing even as she did that it was unreasonable and irrational.

And that was when she figured it out.

The idea of Brady not wanting to be married to her smacked of Dwight again and was pushing those buttons in her. So of course it made her feel bad. That was all there was to it. It didn't have anything to do with Brady or her attraction to him or even anything to do with the pregnancy or the baby. It was just pouring salt into her old wounds.

So everything was okay, she assured herself.

It wasn't as if any part of her actually wanted to stay married to Brady. It was just those old wounds she was struggling with.

What a relief.

"I figure we'll look for a notary as soon as we get to town," he was saying, the first thing to penetrate her preoccupation. "Might as well get that out of the way."

"Sure," she agreed as if she'd never had another thought on the matter.

But it still tweaked her.

And even believing she understood why now, it didn't feel great.

Maybe because no matter how she looked at it, there were two men in the world who'd made it clear they really *didn't* want to be married to her.

One, a man she'd believed she loved.

The other, the father of her baby—and the sole person who had ever made her feel like a real woman.

* * *

The notary was a tall, thin man with a very bad comb-over and a nose so hooked it looked like a beak. He didn't seem to care what Kate and Brady were signing, once he was satisfied they were aware of the contents of the document themselves and agreeable to it. Then he checked their identification, had them autograph the divorce papers and his record book—complete with the date—and he pressed his seal into the space provided, signed it himself and that was that.

"Well, happy divorce," Brady said on the way out of the notary's office.

"Happy divorce," Kate responded.

"Or at least it will be a divorce when I send the papers to the lawyer and he files them. Feel better?"

Not at all, was what Kate would have said if she were being honest. But she'd been the one to demand this so she could only say, "Yes. You?"

"Sure. Want to know why?"

Maybe not, she thought. But she played along, anyway, as they stepped out into the cool clear air. "Why do you feel better now that the divorce papers are signed? Because you were afraid you were really going to get stuck with me?"

He was looking down at her and he hadn't yet replaced his sunglasses, so she could see in his eyes that that wasn't what he'd been thinking and he was slightly offended that she might believe he had been.

"I feel better because you were so freaked out by this whole thing and I'm hoping now that it's taken care of—basically—maybe we can put it behind us and really start over the way we agreed to do the first night I got to Elk Creek.''

''The clean slate,'' she said, referring to that same night.

''Right.''

''Okay,'' Kate said, but for some reason it didn't seem to appease him, and she had the impression he had something else in mind.

''You know,'' he said. ''We've said we'll be friends and that we'd pretend to go along with some of Matt's maneuverings to get him off our backs, but I'm just thinkin'—what if we really did put some effort into gettin' to know each other? For real. Would that be so bad? I mean, is that just totally what you don't want or could we give it a try?''

Could they? she asked herself. Could they make a genuine effort to really get to know each other?

It was tempting. It was something she realized she wanted to do. But should she? Wasn't it also dangerous, given her already strong attraction to him?

But then it occurred to her that if they were going to have a child—which they were, whether he realized it or not—they were going to need to have a relationship of some kind. Not a romance, because she was convinced that wasn't what she wanted. But at least a friendly, hopefully considerate, compassionate, adult relationship. A relationship in which they knew a little something about each other, if for no other reason than to be able to answer questions their child might pose down the road. And in the interest of that, what he was suggesting seemed like the smart thing to do.

As long as she could keep the whole attraction element out of it.

"Look, if you don't want to, it's okay," he said then, probably because she'd let too much silence pass as she'd pondered his proposal.

"No!" she said in a hurry. "I *do* want to!"

Okay, too eager now.

She toned down the sound of her voice and the feelings that had prompted it. The feelings she was supposed to be keeping at bay.

"I think that's a good idea," she finally assured him in as businesslike a manner as she could muster. "After all, you are Matt's best friend, and you'll probably end up being my next-door neighbor, and we'll both be living in the same small town. What could make more sense than to honestly get to know each other?"

"Maybe not a ringing endorsement of my own merits, but does that mean we have a deal?"

"Yes. Where should we start?"

Brady grinned at her. "Let's not attack it like it's a school assignment. How 'bout if we just relax a little and let it evolve on its own?"

"And in the meantime I can get my shopping done?"

"Absolutely."

"Great."

And with that they launched an afternoon that turned out to be better than Kate had anticipated.

Somehow she'd forgotten why she'd liked Brady so much in Las Vegas. But shopping in Cheyenne reminded her. The plain, undeniable truth was that when she did as he'd advised and relaxed a little, she and Brady clicked on so many levels. More levels than she had remembered from the New Year's trip.

Their senses of humor were similar. Their tastes were similar. Sometimes it even seemed as though they thought the same thoughts at the same time.

And it felt good to temporarily suspend all the weighty issues that she'd been carrying around with her. To revert to the way things had been between them before New Year's Eve. To rediscover not only the fun she had with him, but the fun he brought out in her.

The day was productive in other ways, too. Kate found the perfect leather-bound album for the gift she had planned for her grandfather, and Brady decided to get Buzz a birthday present of his own. He chose a silver belt buckle that Kate knew her grandfather would have picked out for himself if he'd had the chance.

While they were at the Western store buying the buckle, the display of Stetsons caught Brady's eye, and he decided to get himself a new hat. It meant trying on a variety of them—wide-brimmed, narrow-brimmed, felt, leather, even one that looked more like a straw sombrero than a cowboy hat.

But he finally found one that suited him—a buckskin beaver felt with a narrow black leather band—and then went to work with the hat creaser, discussing the subtle differences between a cattleman's crease, a quarter-horse crease and a cutter crease, to decide which would look best on him.

Kate observed that part of the proceedings from a distance, sitting in a barrel chair near the dressing rooms and fighting a laugh at what she was witness to. Because no woman had ever had so serious a deliberation about any form of clothing or hairstyle.

Not that she wasn't enjoying the sight, though, because she was. How could anyone *not* have liked looking at the tall, broad-shouldered cowboy standing with long, thick legs apart, running his fingertips lovingly along the hat brim and tipping it just so on his head?

And she had to admit, the hat did look good on him. Especially once it was finished and had just the right dip to the front brim, giving both man and Stetson a cocky, sexy accent.

But getting to know Brady was one thing. Noticing things like that was another. That was just what she shouldn't be doing, so Kate tried to sigh away the effects.

Just friends, she reminded herself. Just friends...

It was after seven by the time they'd done all they needed to do in Cheyenne and Brady suggested dinner at a steak house, where the food was incredible but the country-western music was so loud they could hardly talk to each other over the noise.

Then they went back to the airport.

"Buckle up, baby, and I'll fly you to the moon,"

Brady joked as they took their seats in his plane again and he did a preflight check.

Kate liked watching that, too. Watching his expertise and seeing the evidence of the fact that he was intelligent as well as gorgeous. Of course, it only mattered to her in terms of the genes he might have passed on to her unborn child, she told herself. It wasn't as if her appreciation had anything to do with him as a man or her as a woman.

Then they were in the air again, and the pitch-blackness of the night sky made her feel as if they were the only two people in the world. Not a feeling she minded, she realized, even though she knew she shouldn't really be indulging in it.

But where was she going to go to stop it?

"You know," Brady said then. "You're wrecking my pilot-and-the-beautiful-but-scared-passenger fantasy."

That made Kate laugh. "I beg your pardon?"

"Well, here I have you all alone, up in the air, and if you had some white-knuckled fear of flying I could be a hero."

"Wouldn't you have to be a *dashing* hero?" she teased him.

"It goes without saying," he said with mock humility. "Did you want to pretend? Say, tremble a little or something, so I could show you my stuff?"

"I don't think I want to see your *stuff*," she said, unintentionally putting some innuendo in that last word.

"But I don't get this chance too often, you know."

"I don't believe that. I'll bet you use this plane as your come-on. Instead of inviting women to your loft to see your etchings, you probably invite them to go flying with you."

He grinned in a way that let her know he'd done exactly that a time or two. "So is that a no? You won't even pretend to be afraid? What if I do this?"

He put the plane into a sharp dip and then yanked it up again.

But Kate took it in stride.

"You're forgetting I have four older brothers," she said, only laughing at his attempt to scare her. "I've been hung by my ankles off the barn roof, taken on every roller coaster they ever got me near, dragged off a cliff by a bicycle while I was wearing roller skates, had to hang on to the hood of a truck for dear life while Matt raced across an open field, been set backward in the saddle of a horse whose rump got slapped so it would run away with me and awakened from a sound sleep to find my nose pressed to the ceiling because they'd put my bed up on stilts. A little air turbulence just won't do it."

He half frowned, half grinned at her. "They did all that to you?"

"And more. Much, much more. I was their own private plaything when it came to practical jokes, pulling the wool over someone's eyes and just plain orneriness."

"That's bad."

"Tell me about it."

"Now I just feel guilty for wanting you even a little nervous."

"Good," she said with a laugh. "Then do something else."

"Like what?"

"Like… Tell me about your family."

"My family," he repeated as if he were trying to come up with something worthy of the telling. "Okay. Well, you know how people say they were childhood sweethearts? That was my folks. My mom's family moved across the street from my dad's family when they were both eight years old. My dad always said he fell in love with my mom the first time he laid eyes on her and it never changed from that minute on."

"What about your mom?"

"She said my dad had cowlicks and his hair stuck up so she thought he was funny looking. But he was tireless in his determination to win her over—"

"At eight?"

"Even at eight. And he didn't give up until he'd done it. But it took until she was nine."

"And they were married at ten?" Kate joked.

"Now that would be too far-out," he deadpanned. "No, they were sweethearts all the way through school and got married the week after they graduated. They were together—happily—until the day they died."

Because neither of them felt trapped, Kate thought, for no reason she understood. But it added strength to her own resolve, anyway.

"How did they die?" she asked more solemnly.

"Car accident. A drunk driver hit them head-on. It's been about three years now. But as bad as it was to lose them like that and so young, my brother and I agreed that it would have been worse to see them go one at a time, later in life. They really were two halves of a whole, and either of them would have been lost without the other."

"So that's what you're looking for, I'll bet—a love like that."

Brady seemed to think about it. Then he chuckled slightly. "I've never looked at it that way."

And maybe he didn't want to look too closely at it that way now, either, because rather than delving into it, he gave her a sideways glance again and said, "What about your folks? I've met them, and Matt's talked about them here and there, but how'd they get together? And wasn't there some problem with Buzz because of it?"

"*Big* problems with Buzz because of it. My parents met at the Stock Show in Denver the winter my mother was seventeen. My dad was twenty. They say it was love at first sight—sort of like your dad, only my dad didn't have cowlicks so my mom was head-over-heels in love with him from the get-go, too. But he lived in Texas and she was still in high school. There was no way Buzz was going to let his only daughter, his only child, drop out of school the way she wanted, to marry some guy who—to make matters worse—would take her off to Texas to live. So they eloped, and my mother didn't have any contact with her parents again until I was seventeen and she started to see things through her father's eyes. Then they reconciled and they've been on good terms ever since. My mother calls Buzz at least once a week now even though she and my father are traveling the country."

"But basically your parents did the Texas-Elk-Creek version of Romeo and Juliet, huh? Sounds like you have some pretty high standards to live up to in the romance department yourself."

"Maybe all that love-at-first-sight business is what got us both to the altar in Las Vegas," she said.

"Maybe. But we wiped that slate clean, remember? We're not talking about it."

"Mmm."

"You're right, though," Brady went on. "When you grow up seeing two people as crazy about each other as my folks were, it's a hard act to follow. You want it for yourself, but sometimes you get to thinking that it just isn't out there for you."

"Are you getting melancholy on me?" she asked, teasing him to ward off feeling exactly that way herself. And for the same reason. She'd always looked at what her parents shared and wished for the same thing. And worried that she wouldn't ever find it.

"Melancholy? Me? Nah. How could I be melancholy with a new hat back there in its own seat?"

Kate laughed, recalling that he'd actually buckled the hat into a seat belt as if it were precious cargo.

Brady concentrated more closely on his flying then, because they'd passed over Elk Creek and were about to land in the pasture his plane had been in since his arrival. He smoothly eased the aircraft to the ground not far from where Matt had left his truck for them to drive back in. Then, when the plane came to a standstill, he cut the engines, and quiet wrapped around them, heralding the end of their trip and their day together.

And Kate felt an awful pang of regret that it was coming to a conclusion.

She fought it, though. Telling herself just how inappropriate the sentiment was under the circumstances she was determined to impose upon them.

They transferred all their packages from the plane to the truck and exchanged small talk on the short drive from the north pasture to the house. No one was in sight when they let themselves in through the kitchen's French doors and they both headed for the hallway that led to their bedroom suites.

From that direction they passed Brady's door first, and he set his hat can down in front of it before taking the remainder of the packages he was carrying for Kate to her room.

"I can take those," she told him when she'd opened her own door, thinking that if she had him bring the bags and boxes into her room, she wouldn't want to let him back out again.

Brady didn't protest, he just handed everything over.

And then there they were, Brady in the hall facing her as Kate stood in the doorway looking up at dark-molasses hair that was a little mussed from all the hat trials, and blue-gray eyes peering down at her from a face that was handsome enough to make her heart skip a beat.

"Thanks. I had a nice day," she said then in a voice that was softer, breathier than she'd wanted it to be.

"First Las Vegas and now Cheyenne—we do know how to do a town up right, you and I, don't we?" he said with a slow smile.

"Cheyenne will never be the same after today," she agreed as if they'd done something wild and woolly rather than merely shop.

But it made his smile grow even wider, and suddenly Kate was all too aware of every inch of the man. Of broad shoulders and solid chest and the whole long length of him standing there in all his masculine glory and that pure sexuality that she could feel in the air around them as sure as if it were a living thing.

He reached a hand to her arm in a gesture that began as no more than any friend touching another friend as he was about to say good-night. But in that instant, when his touch seared through the sleeve of the light sweater she wore, what was ignited inside Kate was something so much more than feelings of friendship. Something warm and full and alive. Something rich with needs and desires and cravings for more.

His smile was gone, replaced by an expression that said he could well be feeling the same things and that he was as taken aback by them, by the speed with which they'd hit, as she was.

But his resistance must not have been any greater, because he raised his other hand to her other arm, and there was most certainly not mere friendship in his drawing her nearer, in adding a little pressure from strong fingers that massaged and caressed and sent glittering shards of light all through her.

Then he bent over just far enough to press his lips to hers, and if his touch alone had awakened things inside her, it was nothing compared to what his mouth against hers inspired.

And this time the kiss wasn't only the brief peck of the previous evening. This time his lips parted over hers. This time he even let them linger long enough for her to savor the soft feel of his mouth, to taste the warm sweetness of his breath, to let her head fall back in surrender to something she knew she should stop but couldn't muster any inclination to—

The sound of voices going into the kitchen from the recreation room drifted to them, and Kate broke away in a hurry.

It appeared as if the sounds from the kitchen penetrated Brady's consciousness only after she'd ended the kiss, and for a moment he seemed slightly crestfallen.

But Kate whispered, "Someone's coming," to let him know that was the reason she'd so abruptly ended what she had really wanted to have go on and on.

Brady nodded with merely the tilt of his chin and

took a big step backward himself, putting distance between them.

But whoever had gone into the kitchen stayed there, never venturing into the portion of the house where Kate and Brady waited to be discovered.

The intimate moment between them had passed, though. And as much as Kate yearned for him to take her in his arms, to kiss her again—and again and again—he didn't do it.

Instead he said a quiet good-night and disappeared with his new hat into his own room.

Kate followed suit, closing her door behind her and then leaning against it, still hanging on to her forgotten packages and reliving that kiss in her mind.

And as surely as she knew she shouldn't have let Brady kiss her again tonight, she also knew that she wished he were right there with her still, kissing her until her lips were numb. Touching her until she tingled all over. Holding her in those enormously strong, powerful arms. Undressing her with deft fingers. Taking her to bed to do those things she only had a blurry memory of from New Year's Eve....

"Friends," she muttered to herself. "We're just going to be friends."

The trouble was, no friend she'd ever had before had made her feel what Brady made her feel. And she wondered how a person took those feelings he brought to life in her and turned them platonic.

Because she was failing miserably....

Chapter Seven

It snowed the next day. One of those heavy, wet snows that pile up on the grassy areas but turn instantly to slush on the pavement and sidewalks. Spring snow.

But it made for the perfect afternoon for Kate to stay inside with Tallie, Maya and Jenn to begin their preparations for Buzz's eightieth birthday party by doing some early decorating of the living room—something they could do since the party wasn't a surprise.

They had the house to themselves. Buzz had gone into town to play cards with his cronies, and the rest of the men in residence—including Brady and little Andrew—were out in the barn.

That meant that Kate and Brady hadn't crossed

paths at all today because he'd already had lunch and gone outside with her brothers and nephew by the time the morning sickness had passed and she'd emerged from her rooms.

She counted avoiding Brady as the one advantage to the illness she was waking up with every day now.

By late in the afternoon the women moved into the kitchen to inventory the ingredients for the food they'd be preparing in the next two days, and to make sure they had enough paper plates and plastic silverware.

As everyone else dealt with the food, Kate took the job of paper plate counter at the center island, facing the French doors that looked out onto the back patio and the barn beyond it. So she was the first to see the men emerge from the barn and go to work on what appeared to be a snow fort for Andrew. Although, it looked as if the little boy was only the outward excuse for the big boys to play in the snow.

But regardless of the reason, Kate found it difficult to tear her eyes off the scene framed by the French doors.

Well, she found it difficult to tear her eyes off one member of the scene framed by the French doors, anyway.

Brady joined in the construction with vigor, and wherever he was at any given moment, Kate's gaze seemed to follow with a will of its own.

He cut quite a figure, there was no denying it. He had on cowboy boots and faded blue jeans that fitted his thick thighs and incredible derriere as if they'd been made by a London tailor. On top he wore layers for warmth—a red Henley T-shirt next to skin she fought not to think about, a chambray shirt over that and a short denim jacket over the shirt.

But even all the clothes couldn't disguise the breadth of straight shoulders or the bulk of biceps or the pure power of his chest. And not even distance diminished Kate's appreciation of it all.

Not that she wasn't looking for a flaw in him, because she was. Anything that might turn the tide for her.

But could she find even one? A repulsive bump in his nose? An unattractive angle to his jaw? That he threw like a girl when the snow fort was built and a snowball fight erupted?

No, she couldn't.

His nose was great. His jaw was sharp and chiseled. And when he threw the snowballs he so expertly packed, he looked like an Olympic athlete.

No matter how hard she tried, there just wasn't anything about him that she could come up with to counteract the undeniable attraction she had to him.

And she was trying. Why else would she have had to count the paper plates three times now?

As she started on the fourth attempt, her sisters-in-law and soon-to-be-sister-in-law caught sight of the antics outside. They all moved to the French doors to watch and joke about the boyishness of their respective men, but Kate stayed where she was, pretending to have no interest in the snowball fight.

But the truth was it wasn't boyishness that kept

her gaze surreptitiously riveted to Brady, that had her subtly altering her stance so she could see him between Maya and Jenn. It was the grace of his movements, the simmering sexuality that seemed to present itself even in his bending over to scoop up snow in big gloved hands. It was the striking curve of his back when he launched his snowy missiles with true aim and the accompanying joyfully wicked smile she'd seen a time or two.

And every return hit he took was evidence of the solid wall of powerful male body that Kate yearned to snuggle up against.

Things would definitely have been easier if he were a gargoyle of a man. Or even if he were just on Dwight's level—okay looking but nothing to turn heads. Plain, really.

But, no, Brady was spectacularly handsome. Spectacularly sexy. Spectacularly man. Way, way more man than Dwight had been.

And she hadn't been woman enough even for Dwight....

That thought made Kate finally able to take her eyes off Brady.

It was good to remember her limitations, she told herself. If she couldn't find a flaw in him, at least she could keep things in perspective by remembering that she was a woman who had a long history of being utterly resistible to the opposite sex. Even to lesser men than Brady.

Yes, perspective, that was important. Keep things in perspective, she reaffirmed. Because pregnant or

not, Brady was out of her league. Far out of her
league. It was something she had a lifetime of evidence to fall back on.

Brady might have had a little bit of an attraction
to her—that was something she'd inspired along the
way in several guys. But when it came to more than
that? There just *wasn't* more than that. Not enough
to maneuver through the obstacle course her brothers
had put up all through school. Not enough to hang
on to Dwight. Certainly not enough to have a future
with a man like Brady.

And not to remember that was to risk having unrealistic expectations. Unrealistic expectations that
could get her hurt. Really hurt. The way she'd been
hurt by Dwight. The way she never wanted to be hurt
again.

The way she wouldn't *let* herself be hurt again. No
matter what she had to do to keep it from happening.

"I'm going to get them in here before they're all
sopping wet," Tallie said then, her voice invading
Kate's thoughts.

Kate's sister-in-law opened the French doors and
shouted for the snow warriors to come in and have
hot cocoa.

Kate took that as her cue to escape back to her
rooms before she ended up any nearer to Brady and
the potency of his effect on her. Better to avoid the
potency of that effect when she knew she didn't have
that same potent effect on him.

So as men and boy brushed the snow off before
heading for the house, she announced that she had

to make a phone call to her contractor and slipped out of the kitchen.

And with her she took her lowered expectations, the recognition of her limitations and that newfound perspective, wrapping it all around her like a suit of armor.

Dinner that night—like every other meal when so many of the McDermots were in attendance—was a noisy affair. Kate didn't mind. It was fun, and being among so many other people made it somewhat easier for her to keep some control over the onslaught of things Brady stirred up in her.

When everyone had finished eating and the kitchen was cleaned, she excused herself and holed up in the den with a box of old photographs and a second box that contained mementos, both of which she wanted to go through.

She was congratulating herself on making it for a whole day without being alone with Brady when he knocked on the door and poked his head in.

"Hey, stranger. I was wonderin' where you'd gone off to. You avoidin' me today?"

"Didn't we just have dinner together?" she countered, playing innocent.

"We had dinner in the same room, but I don't think you could say we had it *together*." He poked his chin in her direction. "What're you up to?"

"Is Buzz within earshot?"

Brady reared back enough to look around then

slipped into the den and closed the door behind him. "All clear. Is this top secret?"

It didn't take more than his entrance to make the air in the room seem charged. And as much as Kate knew she should do her best to get rid of him and continue her reprieve from what he did to her insides every time he got near her, the excitement he brought in with him was intoxicating and left her knowing she wouldn't do any such thing.

Instead she said, "I'm putting my gift to Buzz together."

"Is that so?" Brady strolled to the leather sofa where she sat with a few pictures already on the coffee table in front of her and a roaring fire in the fireplace nearby. "And what exactly is your present going to be?" he asked.

"You know I bought the album in Cheyenne yesterday. I thought I'd turn it into a sort of scrapbook for him. Since he wasn't a part of our lives until we were all basically grown-up, he missed our childhoods. So I'm going to use pictures of Shane and Ry and Bax and Matt and me when we were kids and a few keepsakes—ribbons we won, things like that."

"Nice," Brady said, infusing the single word with sincerity. "Can I help?"

"I don't know how. I just need to go through all the old pictures and things and decide what I want to use."

"Then can I just look at the old pictures while you do? I'm a sucker for stuff like that."

She couldn't come up with a reason why he

shouldn't see the photographs, so she said, "Sure. Okay. If you want."

If he heard the lack of enthusiasm in her voice he ignored it. Instead he sat beside her on the couch. So close beside her that his thigh brushed hers and suddenly made the jeans she had on feel as warm as a heating pad.

Great. Now he's giving me hot pants, she thought, wishing his nearness didn't feel good enough to want to lean in even closer to him.

As usual he smelled wonderful. Apparently he'd shaved before supper, and that clean scent only added to the headiness she'd been feeling ever since he'd come in.

How was she supposed to fight the emotional effects of the man, she wondered, when there were so many physical effects to go along with them? It was a double whammy.

"I thought I'd start with pictures of us as babies, maybe put them around a snapshot of the ranch we grew up on in Texas since Buzz never got down there to see the place," Kate said as they began to sort through the photographs that were merely thrown haphazardly into a toaster-size box. "Then I'll try to work my way up through the years to high school and college graduations, and finish with a picture I had everyone sit for two weeks ago, all of us together."

"Sounds like a good plan," Brady said, studying each photo closely before trading Kate for the ones she took from the box first.

"Here's one of you as a baby," he announced when he happened across a shot of Kate at about four months old, sitting on her mother's lap.

"Are you sure?" she asked as she glanced back and forth between two others to decide which she wanted to use.

"Positive. You're the only McDermot with curly hair and that particular shade of green eyes. Besides, I don't think any of your brothers would have let a picture of them in a pink-flowered dress survive."

Kate took the photograph, verifying that it was indeed her. "That's a good one of me to start out with."

"You were a cute baby."

"All babies are cute."

"Not true. My brother was a homely little cuss. Actually, he was a homely big cuss. Nearly twelve pounds at birth. He looked like a Sumo wrestler."

"Twelve pounds?" Kate repeated in awe tinged with trepidation, hoping her own baby didn't take after its uncle. "What about you?"

"Now I was a beauty," Brady said without skipping a beat.

He made that sound as if he were exaggerating wildly but she couldn't imagine that he'd been anything less than a beautiful baby.

"How big were you?" she asked.

"'Bout nine pounds."

"Wow," Kate breathed. "Your poor mom."

"Mmm," he agreed, obviously not having a clue as to why she was so interested in the subject.

"Here's Ry and Shane," she said then, pulling out a shot of her dad juggling both twins at once.

"Geez, I thought they looked a lot alike now but your folks must have had to mark an A and a B on their bellies when they were born to know which was which."

"Don't worry, they got plenty of mileage out of switching places and fooling people."

Brady laughed out of the blue then but clearly not at what Kate had said. He was staring intently at yet another picture. "What happened to your hair here?"

Kate leaned in slightly to peer at the photograph and felt more of the warmth of Brady's body as she did. She wasn't having much luck not being ultra-aware of every nuance, every tiny effect, almost of every breath he took.

"Oh, that one," she said. "Bax gave me a haircut. Daddy had taken all the boys into the barbershop to have haircuts for Easter, and I was mad because I'd been left out. So Bax did the honors."

"Good thing he didn't become a surgeon," Brady said with another chuckle at the misshapen, lopsided, bald-in-some-spots abomination of a haircut her brother had given her when she was four.

"Better add this to the album. It's too funny to leave out," Brady suggested.

Kate took the picture from him and also lost the excuse to lean against him. Something she regretted more than she'd expected to, when she straightened up.

Maybe he regretted it, too, because he leaned her

way then, renewing the contact, to poke a finger at a picture still in the box rather than pick it up himself.

"Early *Sports Illustrated* swimsuit modeling?" he asked.

Kate lifted the photo out of the box and held it so they could both see it. In the picture she stood on a beach, the ocean behind her, dressed in a two-piece suit. She was all of five or six.

"I was getting some practice," she confirmed in a deadpan.

Brady took the picture from her and looked at it more closely. But only when he ran his thumb over the spot that showed the heart-shaped birthmark she had just above her left hipbone did it occur to her what he was thinking. He'd done that same thing New Year's Eve only on the genuine article when he'd discovered it.

"Your broken heart," he murmured, referring to the fact that although it was an almost perfect heart shape, it was separated directly through the center for about half its length. "I'd forgotten about that."

Among a lot of other things about her and that night that he'd no doubt forgotten about, Kate thought, slightly dejected by the reminder of just how unmemorable she was. Even if there was a whole lot about Brady and that night that *she* didn't recall.

"You said your mother had always told you it was the only broken heart you'd ever know," Brady added then, as if just remembering that now, too.

"How wrong she was," Kate heard herself say before she'd even realized she was going to.

But she didn't want to think about the heartbreak that hadn't been confined to her birthmark. Or talk about it, either.

She also didn't want to go on feeling the way she was feeling, watching Brady caress that spot on the photograph much the way he'd caressed the birthmark itself that other night. She didn't want to go on feeling so warm that the fire suddenly seemed to have been a mistake. Feeling an immense craving to have Brady run that blunt thumb across the birthmark itself again right that minute....

"Here's one of Matt," she blurted out then, nearly shoving another photograph at her brother's friend to distract him from the beach shot. "I think I'll save the swimsuit picture for *Sports Illustrated* when they come calling," she added to let him know it was time to dispose of it.

Brady didn't give up the beach shot easily, but he did finally hand it over to Kate, accepting the picture of his friend instead.

He had a good laugh at Matt in his superhero Halloween costume and that helped to diffuse some of what had been going through Kate, it helped her relax and get back to business.

They spent the rest of the evening that way—looking through the box of photographs and sorting small plastic trophies, award ribbons, report cards and various other keepsakes in the other one.

Somewhere along the way Kate slipped down to

sit on the floor with her back against the front of the sofa.

Somewhere along the way Brady did, too, only he sat on one hip, almost facing her profile, with an arm resting on the couch cushion behind her.

Somewhere along the way they stopped studying pictures and mementos separately and passing them off to each other and instead just checked them out together, usually with Kate holding the item in question and Brady looking on, near enough for her to feel the heat of his breath, to indulge in the scent of his aftershave, to be almost cocooned by his big body.

And somewhere along the way Kate forgot she was supposed to be keeping things in perspective. She forgot her limitations. Forgot everything and started to just have a good time.

She reveled in walking down memory lane with him. In sharing childhood memories and anecdotes with him. In letting him see her family history.

Before either of them realized it, it was midnight and they'd reached the bottom of both boxes. There weren't any other sounds coming from anywhere outside the den, and it seemed apparent that they were the only two still up and about.

Kate had a tall pile of what she'd chosen for the scrapbook, and the remainder they repacked. Then Brady gave a great stretch, raising his long arms into the air and arching his back, and Kate heard his spine crack.

"Ouch. Was that as painful as it sounded?" she asked.

"Nah, felt good."

Well, it *looked* good, too. But she tried not to notice.

When he was through stretching he got to his feet and reached a hand down to help her to hers.

She knew it was a mistake to take it, to allow herself the physical contact that the whole evening had been just short of. But she had to do it. Not only so she wouldn't seem standoffish, but also because she just *had* to do it, because she had to indulge.

So she did, slipping her hand into the undeniable strength of his workman's hand and letting him pull her to stand before him.

For a moment after she got there he looked down into her eyes, and she expected something more to follow. Another kiss maybe?

But rather than that he gave her a mischievous smile and said, "How bad would it be if we got into some of the ice cream for the party?"

"Ooh, bad. Very bad," she said with a voice full of wicked delight just the same.

"Unforgivable?"

"Maybe not *that* bad."

"How 'bout if we figure we'll eat our share tonight and skip it at the party?"

"That seems fair," she finally agreed.

They made their way to the deserted kitchen where they took two gallons of ice cream out of the freezer—one Black Forest and the other plain chocolate.

"I suppose we have to use bowls?" Brady said.

"I think we'd better," Kate confirmed. While she got out the ice cream scoop, he took two bowls from the cupboard and brought them to the island where they each perched on a tall stool and helped themselves to both flavors.

"This is heaven," Brady said rapturously when they dug in.

"Maya's mom made it just for the party."

"Well I'm a connoisseur of ice cream and I can tell you this is fantastic."

"A connoisseur of ice cream, huh? Is that just a nice way of saying you're a glutton?" she teased with a glance at his full bowl.

"I beg your pardon. I spent three summers in high school dishing it out in a little parlor near where I lived."

Kate couldn't suppress a smile. "You were a soda jerk? Did you wear the little hat and a little bow tie and everything?"

"Just a plain white shirt. But I'll have you know that folks came from miles around for my banana splits."

He put a lascivious spin on that and made Kate laugh.

Then he added, as if confiding in her alone, "It was a great way to get girls."

"As if you had problems in that department," she

countered just before eating another spoonful of the icy confection.

"Has Matt been talkin' out of school?"

"As if I couldn't guess," she said, feasting as much on the sight of him as on the ice cream. "I'll bet you collected way more than your fair share of female hearts," she persisted, suddenly wanting very much to know.

"I was pretty lucky with the ladies," he conceded. "'Course it took me until just recently to find out it really had been luck and that that luck could run out."

"When you met me," she said, jumping to the conclusion.

It made him frown slightly. "You make that sound like you're some kind of bad penny. My luck ran out before I met you. Just before, as a matter of fact. Hooking up with you in Vegas... Well, that was the first bright spot I'd had in two months."

Until New Year's morning when I went ballistic, Kate thought. But she didn't say it. Besides not wanting to ruin the mood between them she was more curious about exactly how his luck with the ladies had run out.

"What happened two months before Las Vegas?" she asked.

His eyebrows took loft as he swallowed a mouthful of ice cream. When he had, he said, "Claudia Wence."

He gave the name a dire tone.

"The evil princess?" Kate queried as if they were narrating a cartoon.

Brady chuckled lightly, but somehow she could tell there was nothing light about this subject for him.

"She probably couldn't be called evil, no," he said. "But she was the first woman I'd ever wanted who didn't want me back."

Now it was Kate's turn to raise her eyebrows. "You actually made it to two months before your thirtieth birthday without ever being rejected by a woman?"

He had the good grace to look sheepish. "I know. It's hard to believe. But it's true."

"It's not only hard to believe, it must be some kind of record."

"For the *Guinness* book? I don't think so."

"So what happened?"

"We met in an elevator. Hit it off. She actually asked me out. Very suggestively, in fact. Things went pretty quick—again under her initiative. After about six weeks of seeing each other she moved into my place, started talkin' about our future together. Long-term."

"And that didn't set off any alarms in you? I thought you weren't ready to settle down yet."

"I admit it set off a few alarms, and I was a little worried that she might be rushin' the relationship. But I really cared about her, and it wasn't as if she was talkin' about eloping on the spot or anything. And actually thinkin' about us bein' together down the road felt good."

"So what happened?" Kate repeated.

"Three days before her birthday, at the end of October, she came home and announced as she was packing, that she'd fallen out of love with me—that's what she said. Just like that. With a shrug. As if it were no big deal. She'd met another guy she wanted to date, and she was moving out. So long. It's been fun."

"And you had a rude awakening in the form of your first rejection ever."

"Not only in the form of my first rejection ever, but also in the form of how hard it was to take."

"It's never easy."

"Well it nearly wiped me out. I didn't even know myself for a while."

"And then you met me when you were on the rebound."

He flinched. "That sounds so bad. And not like anything that was goin' on in my head at the time."

"Oh? What *was* going on in your head at the time?"

He grinned that devil's grin that delighted her for no reason she could name. "At first I was thinkin' damn Matt and his matchmakin', and that I'd just like to run the other way because getting involved with my best friend's little sister seemed like the fastest route to ruinin' that friendship."

Kate nodded her understanding. She had a lot of experience with men shying away from her because of her brothers.

"But then when I laid eyes on you," Brady continued, "I was thinkin' that you have hair like winter wheat on a sunny day and eyes the green of the ocean far out to sea and a body that wasn't half-bad, either."

"A body that wasn't *half-bad?* Now there's faint praise."

He grinned the devil's grin again, letting her know he was teasing her with understatement. Then he nudged the air with his chin. "What'd you think of me?"

Oh, good, turn-about. But Kate knew she had that coming.

"I thought you were tall," she said, dealing out some teasing of her own as she took their bowls to the sink and rinsed them.

Brady came to stand beside her at the sink, leaning his hips against the counter's edge. "Talk about faint praise."

Kate put the bowls in the dishwasher and headed for the light switch and the hall that led to their rooms. As she did she said, "I thought you looked like you had a nice personality, too."

Brady laughed quietly as they headed down the hall so as not to disturb anyone behind the other doors they passed. "Try to keep the compliments to a minimum so I don't get a big head," he said facetiously.

They had reached her door by then, and Kate turned to smile at him, unable to resist the opening to tease him yet again by purposely misinterpreting his words. "No, I didn't think your head was too big. Your feet though, those are a different story."

"You're just being mean now."

She decided to cut him some slack. "I thought you had great hair," she said, looking up at the dark, dark fullness of it. "And great eyes," she added before she realized she was going to, as those blue-gray depths caught and held hers.

Then he smiled and stretched the smile into baring his very white, straight teeth. "And how 'bout my choppers? Did you think they were okay?"

"Pretty okay," she confirmed in a voice that had somehow grown breathy when she meant for it to still be teasing him.

He moved his jaw back and forth. "And how 'bout my strong chin? Did you notice that?"

Kate laughed lightly. "Now you're just fishing for flattery."

"True. But remember, I've recently had my ego damaged. It could use some boosting."

"I think it's had all the boosting it needs."

He smiled down at her again, but this time it was sweet and warm and it seemed to wrap her in a golden glow.

"Well, maybe not *all* it needs," he said in an oh-so-quiet, sexy voice.

He went on looking into her eyes, his own alight with mischief and that special brand of life that seemed to shine there. And then his hands were at her shoulders and he'd leaned forward just a bit, enough to let her know he was going to kiss her.

He didn't make any sudden moves, though, so she had the time and opportunity to say no if she didn't want him to.

But she *did* want him to, she realized, and so she didn't move away. In fact, she tilted her own chin in invitation and let her eyelids drift closed just as his mouth met hers.

Only this time—unlike the kisses he'd given her the last two times—it was a kiss to knock her socks off. A kiss with his arms around her. With his fingers kneading her back. With his lips parted and urging hers to part, too. With his tongue coming to call, tentatively at first, the tip barely tracing the sensitive inner rims of her lips, then trailing along the very edges of her teeth, then finding its way inside, finding the tip of her tongue to say hello. To invite it to play. Teaching her the warm, slippery feel. Instigating games that courted and seduced and began to erupt sparkling things inside her.

Her arms were around him, too. Although she wasn't quite sure how or when they'd gotten there. But still her hands filled themselves with the hardness of his back, and one even rose to the nape of his neck where soft bristles of his hair seemed incredibly intimate.

Her breasts were pressed to his chest and she felt her nipples harden, yearning to be noticed, to be paid some attention as her mouth opened wide in response to his and their kiss went to a new, deeper, more passionate level.

And suddenly Kate could only think of pulling

him into her room. Of the fact that her bed was waiting just a short distance away. Of making love with him the night through and replacing the foggy images and unclear memories she had of losing her virginity with him in Las Vegas with the bright, vivid images and memories they could create tonight....

But that was when she recalled they'd already created something. And that at the end of this night— no matter how she spent it—she'd wake up obviously ill as a result of that creation, and Brady would have to know what was going on.

Not to mention that pulling him to her bed, only to have him find out at the end of their night together that she was pregnant, would seem too much like luring him to the trap she didn't want him to ultimately see this baby as.

So she forced herself not to pull him into her room the way she was picturing in her mind, the way she was itching to do. But to push him away instead. To stop the kiss. To step back as if it wasn't what she wanted. To hide the fact that she really wanted so much more.

"Maybe we should say good-night," she told him in a raspy voice that seemed to give her away.

Brady looked down at her from beneath a frown, with an expression on his handsome face that she couldn't read.

But there was too much chaos in Kate to delve into it. She just needed to escape to the safe confines of her room before her tenuous resolve disappeared and she yanked him in with her after all.

"Okay," he agreed in a husky, reluctant voice.

"Good night, then," she said firmly, stepping into her doorway.

"'Night," he answered softly. So softly she couldn't help thinking that it was probably the way he would have said it at the end of hours of lovemaking when they were both exhausted and falling asleep in each other's arms....

But thoughts like that didn't do her any good, and she pushed them aside, grasping the edge of the door as if it were a lifeline and beginning to ease it shut.

"See you tomorrow," she said, so he knew it was coming and it wasn't as if she were closing the door in his face, even though he was still standing there, studying her.

"Yeah," he responded, sounding maybe a little crestfallen. Or did he sound angry maybe? Or disappointed?

She wanted to tell him not to be any of those things, but she couldn't do that any more than she could drag him into her room, to her bed.

So instead she whispered another "Good night" and really did close the door between them.

But not even that solid oak panel could take away what she was feeling.

And what she was feeling was that every inch of her body was alive with wanting the man who was her baby's father.

The very man she couldn't have.

Chapter Eight

Apparently, once the Bartons made up their minds to sell their ranch they didn't want to waste any time. Because Brady got word the next morning that his offer had been accepted.

He arranged to meet the local lawyer who was handling the sale at the Barton place after breakfast to sign some papers, and once he'd had a hearty meal of waffles, eggs and sausages with the McDermot men, he decided to walk across the fields to keep the appointment.

It was a hike of a little over two miles from one door to the other, and he could have driven Matt's truck. Matt had offered it. But after the previous day's snow, the sun was bright in a crystal-clear blue sky, and Brady opted to walk because it seemed like a good chance to clear his head.

And he desperately needed to clear his head. But not of thoughts of buying the Barton ranch. That whole deal had gone through with surprisingly little thought. Instead his mind was filled with something completely different.

It was filled with Kate McDermot. And since talking about Claudia the night before, it was also filled with the reminder that had been.

A reminder that had stayed with him all through the night. A reminder that was still with him this morning.

A reminder about what had gone on with him after Claudia had bailed on him.

He'd gone into some kind of conquest mode that had come out of an obsession to get her back. He wasn't proud of it, but that was how it was.

He'd kept calling her, sending her e-mails, sending her flowers, gifts, messages through friends. He'd put all his energy into wooing her in any way he could come up with.

Just recalling it all now made his hackles rise.

At the time it had seemed like he was meeting a challenge. As if that was all it would take to win her back. But that hadn't been how things were, and he'd had to finally face the fact that her feelings for him weren't the same as his feelings for her. Regardless of what she'd said or how she'd acted before the breakup. And in retrospect it felt degrading to have gone to such lengths for a woman who hadn't wanted him.

Sure, he'd finally come to the point where he was over her, but what he'd gone through before that was something he never wanted to do again. What he needed to think through as he walked across the open fields that separated the McDermot ranch house from the house that would be his, was whether or not that might be happening again, with Kate, even though he didn't want it to.

He wasn't in the midst of the same kind of full-court press, he knew that. But in a more subtle way he was sort of wooing her. And not without what seemed to be some reluctance on her part.

Okay, so there wasn't *total* reluctance on her part the way there had been on Claudia's once she'd moved out. But still, Kate was sending mixed messages. Running hot one minute and cold the next. Which to Brady meant that she had more reluctance to have anything to do with him than he had about having anything to do with her.

Who was he kidding? he asked himself. He didn't feel reluctant at all. Much as he wished he did. Much as he knew it would be better if he did. But instead he actually wanted to be with her. Despite trying to fight it.

And he was trying to fight it. Not successfully, but...

Well, hell, how was he supposed to fight it when he was in the throes of a potent, powerful, red-hot attraction?

A potent, powerful, red-hot attraction that kept her on his mind almost every waking hour? That made him want to spend his every waking moment with her, that had made him go searching for her after supper the night before when he'd known he should just accept that she'd gone on about her business without him? A potent, powerful, red-hot attraction that made being with her for hours seem like mere minutes, that made him want it never to end.

So, no, fighting the drive to be with her, to get to know her, to woo her, wasn't doing much good.

But at the same time he also couldn't help worrying that he could very well be pursuing another woman who didn't want him. Because when Kate was running cold, that was the impression he had. And that was how every meeting with her began.

Sure, she seemed to have a good time when they were together. But at the start it always seemed as if she didn't really want to be with him. As if she was actually avoiding him. Hell, she was as skittish as a colt.

Granted it wasn't as bad as New Year's morning. Or as bad as Claudia's rejection. But it was still there—that feeling that she'd rather not be with him. That he made her uncomfortable for some reason he couldn't figure out. That he was thwarting some plan to keep away from him.

So why didn't he just keep away from her? he asked himself. The way he should have kept away from Claudia.

But that was where things got dicey for him. Because besides the potent, powerful, red-hot attraction that was driving him, she always warmed up once he got past that first hurdle. More than warmed up if you counted last night's kiss. Because that kiss in particular had sure as hell not been cold.

No siree. She'd been as involved in that kiss last night as he'd been. She'd been kissing him back. She'd had her arms around him. Her hands in his hair. There was no mistaking that and he'd thought, It's okay, this is nothing like Claudia....

Until Kate had put a stop to it and acted as if kissing him wasn't what she'd wanted at all.

Hot and cold.

And he'd thought, What the hell am I doing feeling the things I'm feeling, doing the things I'm doing, if she doesn't want it just as much as I do?

Brady shook his head and kicked a fair-size rock with some vengeance.

If she were someone else, he might have thought she was playing games with him. But he didn't have that sense about her. Instead it was as if she were torn, now that he thought about it.

But why would she be? Either she liked him or she didn't.

Unless she really didn't but good manners were behind her being outwardly friendly and polite once she was with him. Good manners that forced her to be pleasant when she really would prefer he keep his distance from her.

But if that was the case, those were some kind of amazingly good manners that had her kissing him the way she had. And he didn't believe anybody had manners *that* good.

Nah, something was definitely going on with her. He just didn't know what it was. And he might never know. So if he had any brains he'd just let her be, he told himself. Better that than risk looking back on this the way he looked back on Claudia, disgusted with himself for putting effort into something he should have walked away from.

"So do it," he said out loud, his words crisp and clear in the silence of the open countryside. "Just cool it with her. Better safe than sorry. Red-hot attraction or no red-hot attraction."

The only problem was that he wasn't sure he could just let her be. Because here it was, ten o'clock in the morning, and he was already champing at the bit to see her again, wondering if she'd be at lunch, thinking about how to get her alone later on.

"Just let'r be!" he shouted at the sky.

But a quiet little voice in the back of his head told him that wasn't going to happen. Not as long as every time he looked at her something in his chest ached. Not as long as every time he heard her voice it made his heart smile. Not as long as every time she laughed he felt like a kid on Christmas morning.

He guessed he just had to hope that what was causing these feelings in him was causing something similar in her and that he wasn't chasing after the unattainable, because Kate was triggering that conquest mode in him again.

And in the meantime, he also had damn sure better

not forget about or discount her reaction to him the morning after they'd made love in Las Vegas. Along with keeping his eyes and ears open so he didn't get in too deep and end up finding himself in the same kind of pain he'd felt with Claudia.

Kate needed to make a trip into Elk Creek that afternoon to check the progress of the remodel of her office. Junebug needed a few last-minute items for Buzz's birthday party the next night, so Kate drove them both into town.

Their first stop was the general store and then they went two doors down to the small corner building Kate had rented, where the contractor worked with two of his men on her bathroom, and Junebug's son Jace was building Kate bookcases that filled a whole wall, floor to ceiling and end to end.

Carpentry wasn't Jace's main employment. He and four of his five brothers ran the family ranch—a smaller spread than many in Elk Creek, so most of the Brimley men also did odd jobs for extra money. When Kate had seen Jace's handiwork on the bookcases in the den, she'd asked Junebug if he would consider doing some for her office, too.

Jace, like all of Junebug's boys—as Junebug still referred to her grown sons—was a mountain of a man and as handsome as they came. It was something Kate hadn't overlooked since moving to Elk Creek and meeting them.

But today it struck another chord in her when she realized that in spite of how bowl-her-over handsome

Jace was, the only thing that came to mind when she first looked at him was that it didn't cause her heart to flip-flop the way every glance at Brady did.

It was disconcerting. Especially because just today she'd ordered herself all over again to get some control over her attraction to Brady so she could deal sensibly with what she needed to deal with. But how successful was she being at that when the sight of another gorgeous hunk of man only made her pine for Brady?

"What do you think?" Jace Brimley asked after he'd greeted his mother and Kate.

Of course he meant what did Kate think about the bookcase, but what went through her mind was, What I think is that I'm in trouble with Brady Brown in more ways than one.

She could hardly say that, though, so instead she said, "They're beautiful."

They were, too. Jace had used solid oak and turned all the edges to give them a fancy finishing touch.

"I have a little more sanding to do, then I'll stain and seal the wood and you'll be all set."

"I can't tell you how much I appreciate this."

"My pleasure," he answered with a warm smile that would have made any woman's knees melt.

But Kate smiled back, feeling absolutely nothing except a desire to hurry home to see Brady.

Oh, yeah, she was definitely in double trouble.

"Will you be home for supper tonight?" Junebug asked her son then.

"Sure. I don't have any other plans," he answered.

"Don't be late," she ordered, and then Junebug marched out the door, ending the visit without another word.

Kate just shrugged as if to say, *I guess that means we're leaving,* said goodbye to Jace and followed the large woman out onto the brick-paved sidewalk where Junebug was surveying the office.

"Glass's broken," the imposing three-hundred-pound Amazon of a woman informed Kate when she joined her.

Kate's glance followed Junebug's pointing finger until she finally spotted what couldn't have been more than a hairline crack of about two inches in the uppermost corner of the picture window.

"Good grief, how'd you ever find that? You must have eagle eyes," Kate said as they both got in her car parked nose-first at the curb.

"I got eyes all right," Junebug assured her, buckling her seat belt. "Speakin' of which, how long you been in the family way?"

Kate felt the color drain from her face. "Excuse me?" she said, glancing at Junebug.

Junebug arched a brow at her. "Got me six sons. Six times I was in the family way. I know it when I see it."

Kate put her eyes on the road and headed out of town, debating about what to do now. But there wasn't an ounce of doubt in the other woman's tone, and in the end Kate simply said, "No one else knows, do they?"

"Not likely. Not that I've heard anybody say. Just you and me. Or does the daddy know, too?"

"No!" Too quickly. Too panicky. Kate took a breath and tried to calm herself down. "I didn't think anyone but me knew. And I just found out a little while ago."

"How far along are you?"

"Slightly over two months."

"And sicker'n a dog every morning. That's why you never come out of your room till noon."

"Is it that obvious?"

"Only to me. Everybody else thinks you're just sleepin' in."

"I wish that was all I was doing," Kate groaned.

"Not a lot of help for it. Tried crackers on your night table?"

"That's usually the first thing to come up."

"My Jace did that to me. Hard on ya."

"Mmm," Kate agreed.

"Helped havin' a husband there by my side."

Kate had been enjoying having someone to talk to about the pregnancy. But it ended with that.

"Where's the daddy?" Junebug asked bluntly.

Kate just shook her head, keeping her eyes on the road.

But Junebug took that the wrong way. "You don't know who the daddy is?"

"No! I mean, I know who he is. But *he* doesn't know."

Junebug nodded, pondering something before she said, "Two months gone—back to February, back to January… Ahh, that explains a lot."

"Excuse me?" Kate repeated.

"That trip to Las Vegas you all had such a good time on. Matt's friend Brady was there, too, if I'm not mistaken. Seems I recall hearin' how the two of you hit it off then."

"Junebug—"

"That's why you're actin' so funny around 'im now, isn't it? He's the daddy."

"Junebug—"

"When're you gonna tell 'im?"

Again, denying anything seemed futile, so Kate didn't try. Instead she said, "Soon."

But that must not have satisfied Junebug because she said, "You are gonna tell 'im, though. Man has a right to know."

Spoken like the mother and champion of six sons.

"Yes, I'm going to tell him. I'm just waiting for the opportune moment." She didn't think she needed to compound things by telling Junebug about the Elvis-impersonator wedding she was waiting to have dissolved first. But she did add, "I don't want him to get the wrong impression."

Junebug laughed out loud at that. "What wrong impression would that be?"

Kate sighed. "I don't want him to think I want anything from him."

"Like marriage."

"Like marriage."

"In my day a man did right by a woman he got in the family way or he wasn't no kind of man at all."

"What if the man were one of your sons now, though?" Kate challenged.

"He'd do right," Junebug answered without skipping a beat.

"And if doing right meant a loveless marriage that made him feel trapped?"

"I'd remind 'im that he liked 'er well enough to diddle with 'er in the first place and tell 'im to go from there lookin' for love. It could come. I've seen it happen."

"And you'd want that for your son? Even if love never did happen and he just always felt trapped and resentful?"

"Babies need a momma and a daddy," Junebug decreed.

"But not necessarily married to each other or living together."

Kate could feel the weight of Junebug's disapproval. But she ventured a question, anyway. "They would feel trapped, wouldn't they? I know my brothers would. I've heard them say it about other men who've been in this situation."

"Is that what you set out to do? Trap 'im?" Junebug asked, rather than answer Kate's question.

"I didn't *set out* to do anything. It just happened."

"And he did his fair share of willingly participatin'? Of chasin' and persuadin' and seducin'?"

"Yes. It wasn't as if I lured him into my bed."

"Then maybe he's more willin' than you think. Seems to me he likes you well enough."

"Liking me well enough and getting all the way to the altar are not the same things. Believe me, I know from experience."

"Could be different with this man," Junebug offered.

"How could it be different with this man when *I'm* not different?" Kate said quietly as she pulled up in front of Junebug's house. "There's already been one man who didn't want me, and that was before, when things were a whole lot less complicated and he'd put in a whole lot more time on a relationship with me. Now, with Brady, who I barely know—"

"Now you're carryin' this man's baby, though."

"That only makes me less appealing."

"Maybe you should let him be the judge of that."

And when Brady himself judged her even less appealing—the way Dwight had? How much would that hurt?

"You didn't answer my question before," Kate reminded Junebug then, for some reason feeling driven to hear what the other woman had to say on the subject. "Don't you think your sons would feel trapped?"

The stern older woman still didn't answer right away. In fact, she waited so long, Kate started to think she couldn't bring herself to.

Then Junebug finally said, "Maybe. Some."

And even though it confirmed exactly what Kate thought, it didn't make her feel any better to hear it.

"But they'd deal with it," Junebug added with conviction. "They'd still have to be told what was goin' on."

"I'm going to tell him. Eventually. But I wouldn't marry him even if he asked. He'd only be asking out of some sense of duty. And it would be a mistake."

Junebug scowled at her, full-bore.

Kate pretended not to notice.

"And please, this is just between you and me," she added.

"No it ain't. This is just between you and the daddy," Junebug amended. "But nobody'll hear it from me, if that's what you're sayin'."

"That's what I'm saying."

But still Junebug sat there, staring at Kate. Then she said, "One of my boys was the daddy, I'd trust 'im to do right *and* to handle any kind of feelin's that came along with it."

Kate just nodded in response to the advice that statement seemed to hold, even if she didn't agree with it.

Apparently Junebug didn't have anything more to say on the subject, so she got out of the car and headed up the walk to her house, again not bothering with a goodbye.

Kate drove off, wishing the older woman had said something to convince her that things might work out for her.

But she'd only helped convince her that what Kate

had thought before was true and that there was no way Brady wouldn't feel trapped when he found out she was pregnant.

No matter how toe-curling that kiss they'd shared the night before had been.

But it was good to have her theory reaffirmed, she told herself. Especially now.

Because after that kiss she'd had a hard time not entertaining fantasies about happy families. About happy futures. About things she wasn't going to have with Brady. And talking to Junebug reminded her that they really were only fantasies and that she'd better not lose sight of what the reality was.

Unfortunately that was easier said than done.

Particularly when she found herself in a lonely bed wishing Brady were there with her....

Chapter Nine

It was a little after five o'clock when Kate got home from dropping off Junebug. She parked her car in the garage out back and crossed the patio to go in through the kitchen doors. But as she approached them she had second thoughts.

She could see through the glass, and what she saw was Brady alone in the expansive, well-appointed room, doing something at the island counter.

He looked as terrific as always, dressed in boots, tight jeans that hugged his narrow hips and thick thighs, and a gray Henley T-shirt that cupped every muscle of his torso and biceps and exposed his forearms where the sleeves were pushed up to his elbows.

She was curious about what he was doing, but just

seeing him from that distance was enough to make her pulse race and her knees go weak. So she decided it was better to walk around to the outside door of her own sitting room and go in that way. At least then she could avoid running into him until supper time.

But just as she was going to alter her direction and head for the side of the house, he looked up as if his radar had been alerted and spotted her.

She knew she'd look foolish if she merely waved and still went around to the other door, so she had to finish her original course and go in through the kitchen.

"Hi," Brady greeted as she came in.

"Hi," she responded, catching his quick head-to-toe once-over that took in her tan slacks and the red cardigan sweater she wore buttoned up the front.

"What are you doing?" she asked with a nod in the direction of the butcher's-block top of the island counter where his massive hands adeptly wielded a knife to slice water chestnuts.

"I'm making rumaki. Maya put a roast in the oven for dinner, but it won't be ready for a couple of hours yet. Everybody's hungry so I thought I'd do a few hors d'oeuvres to tide us over."

"Rumaki?" Kate repeated. "What is that?"

"Classically it's water chestnuts and chicken livers wrapped in bacon, but I'm not big on the chicken livers so I just use the water chestnuts. I marinate them in port wine, then wrap them in the bacon and broil them until the bacon is crisp."

"Ah," Kate said, trying to keep her surprise at this heretofore unseen side of him out of her tone. But she could only accomplish so much. "You cook?"

"Yes, ma'am. I have a pan comin' out of the top oven over there before too long. Sit and visit a few minutes and you can see for yourself."

Kate sat all right. She perched on one of the bar stools across from him even though she knew she should make up some excuse and retreat before that potent charm of his seeped in and left her even more susceptible to him. But he'd really roused her curiosity now. Not to mention that there was a fascination in watching his big hands so adeptly and expertly fashioning the small appetizers.

"None of my brothers cook much," Kate said then. "They can heat up whatever Junebug tells them to and make coffee and cereal, but that's about it."

"Guess you either like to or you don't. I started likin' it in college."

There was a mischievous half grin and a double entendre to that, but Kate pretended not to catch either one. "When you were on your own for the first time and had to cook or starve?" she guessed.

"No, when I went away to a college that cost more than my folks could afford. I needed to work to help with my tuition. My uncle owned a restaurant not far from school so he hired me. I was a busboy to start out. Planned to be a waiter once I learned the ropes, but for some reason the cookin' part of things got me interested and I ended up doin' that instead.

Maybe it harked back to my soda jerk days, fixin' malts and banana splits.''

"What kind of restaurant did your uncle own?"

"Semifancy. Not four-star but not a burger grill or a diner, either. Appetizers, steaks, chops, lobster, a few pasta dishes. My specialty was a blackened pork tenderloin that I came up with. It was a big seller. It'd melt in your mouth. And then of course there were some fancy desserts.''

"You bake, too?" More surprise echoed in her voice.

"No, that's the one thing I didn't get into. The pastry chef was a little toad who was afraid somebody would steal his secrets. I steered clear of him. But I did everything else at one time or another before I finished college.''

"A rancher, a pilot, a soda jerk, a chef—what haven't you done?"

"Brain surgery," he joked, crossing to the oven to open the door so he could peer in at his rumaki.

The smell of bacon cooking hadn't been too strong in the big kitchen until he opened the oven door. But it hit Kate full force then.

Ordinarily it was a smell she liked. But this time it made her stomach lurch. The way her stomach lurched every morning now even without provocation.

She swallowed hard and fought it. This hadn't happened anytime after noon before. Why now?

She got up and poured herself a glass of water from a pitcher in the fridge, breathing deeply of the cold, clearer air that came out with it until she managed some control over the sickness. Then she went back to the bar stool at the island counter about the same time Brady returned there, too.

"You don't look so good all of a sudden," he observed with a concerned frown creasing his brow.

"No. No, I'm fine," she said too quickly, realizing after the fact that she could have lied and said she might be getting the flu. But her immediate thought had been that to admit she was ill at all was to give herself away.

Brady's frown deepened with doubt. "Are you sure my cookin' isn't botherin' you?"

"No, why would it? I like bacon." Although at that moment just the thought of it threatened to make her gag.

She took a sip of her water and turned the subject back to him. "And here I thought you just flew planes."

"Well that is my first love."

"How did you get hooked on that?"

"My dad. He was a plane fanatic from way back. He got my brother and I nutty for them by the time we were knee high. The three of us would build model airplanes together and fly the remote-control kind. Dad'd take us to every air show to come around. But that was where it stopped for Dad and Jack—a hobby. They didn't have the bug I did to actually pilot one myself. So after college I joined the air force and got myself into flight school. Flew jets eventually."

Kate was getting an image of Brady that she hadn't had before. "So you're not the kind of person who could be content sitting on the sidelines or working on the peripheries, are you? You're a doer."

He inclined his head and chuckled a little. "I guess you could say I'm always in the thick of things, yeah."

"A man of action. Better off without ties that bind." Like unplanned parenthood. "You must like having a lot of options."

He laughed at that. "*Everybody* likes having a lot of options."

Another wave of nausea took Kate by surprise just then, strong enough to bring her fingertips to her lips as if that would stop the inevitable.

She swallowed hard and fought the rise of her gorge once more, this time under Brady's watchful eye, his handsome face again pulled into the deeply etched lines of an alarmed frown.

"Are you sure you're okay?"

She nodded, wondering why she was torturing herself by staying in the fumes of that bacon.

But she just couldn't seem to make herself leave.

When she had things settled some, she seized her earlier thought about a way of explaining the sickness and said, "Maybe I'm getting a touch of the flu."

"Maybe you should go lie down."

It was the perfect opportunity to end their conversation and seek the solace of her room. But she was enjoying his company too much—*again*—to do the smart thing.

So instead she took another sip of her water and said, "I'm fine." Then she went back to their former subject. "Have you ever flown commercial jets?"

It took a moment of his scowling scrutiny before he accepted that she didn't want to talk about the way she was feeling and answered her question.

"I flew for a small airline for about a year, just long enough to save up the down payment on my own plane. Then I did charters and crop dusting. I like being my own boss."

"Footloose and fancy-free," she supplied.

"On the work front, anyway," he agreed. "That's why I figured investing in a ranch was a good way for me to go. I can run my own place and hire out for dustin', too."

Kate nodded, still trying to will this new bout of sickness to pass.

Why now? she asked herself again. Wasn't it bad enough to wake up this way every morning? Did it have to assault her in the middle of the day, too? In front of someone else? In front of Brady, of all people?

The oven timer went off then, and Brady retraced his steps to open the door again.

And once more the bacon smell intensified. In fact, it seemed overwhelming.

Kate took another sip of her water, marveling at how something as simple as a common scent could do this to her. Maybe she was just imagining it, she told herself. Maybe if she practiced a little mind over matter she could conquer it.

"All done," Brady said, using a dish towel to protect his hands as he pulled out the cookie sheet full of rumaki and brought it with him to set down on the island counter. Directly in front of Kate.

Mind over matter was not succeeding as she looked down at the small hors d'oeuvres, the bacon still sizzling in little puddles of its own grease.

And never had she seen anything more stomach churningly unappealing.

The smell was all around her now. Inescapable. Awful. Overpowering.

Overpowering enough that she knew she wasn't just imagining the sickness that was gaining a rapid stronghold as surely as it did every morning, mind over matter or no mind over matter.

And this time when her hand went to her mouth it wasn't merely a reflex in response to a wave of simple nausea.

It was a necessity as she ran like mad for the nearest bathroom.

Kate woke up an hour later. She'd been sick so many times she'd lost count before succumbing to the accompanying exhaustion and falling asleep on the bed.

She felt better, though. In fact she felt just fine. Fine enough to even be hungry, although she was leery of leaving her rooms and rediscovering the bacon smell and the sickness all over again.

She got up and went to the sink in the bathroom, grimacing at the first sight of herself in the mirror above it.

Her mascara had melted into black crescents beneath both eyes, her skin was pale and her hair was a total mess. If she decided to venture out of her rooms for something to eat she couldn't do it looking like that, she decided. So she brushed her teeth thoroughly, washed her face and brushed her hair into a curly top-knot held at her crown with an elastic scrunchee.

Vanity took hold from there and she reapplied mascara and blush because she couldn't stand the thought of encountering Brady without it—crazy as she knew that was.

Her clothes still bore a faint trace of the bacon smell, so she stripped them off and went to the closet for something fresh. Opting for comfort over fashion, she chose a black fleece jumpsuit and slipped into it, appreciating the downy-softness of its inside against her bare skin since she'd even shed her bra, figuring the two large pockets over each of her breasts allowed for enough camouflage to allow that.

There was a knock on the sitting-room door as she pulled the zipper up the front, stopping a few inches below the hollow of her throat.

Brady was waiting in the hallway when she opened the door, bearing a tray and a surprised expression as his gaze took her in.

"Wow. Now there's an improvement," he said in greeting.

Kate smiled, glad she'd gone to the trouble of cleaning up.

"You seem to have made a miraculous recovery," he added.

"I have. I fell asleep and when I woke up a few minutes ago I felt perfectly fine again," she explained. "Must have been a fast-moving flu."

"I knew you were asleep. I came to check on you and when there was no answer to my knock I sent Maya in to see if you were okay. She said you were asleep and we all decided it was probably better to leave you alone. I've been listening for sounds of life since then, and when I heard them I fixed you tea and toast in case you felt up to it." He raised the tray slightly to indicate that was what was on it.

Kate appreciated the gesture. And the care and nurturing that came with it. "Tea and toast, huh?" she said, craning forward to peer at the contents of the tray.

"I can get you something else if you're hungry. Just not rumaki."

Kate wrinkled her nose at the mere mention of the word. "Definitely not rumaki. I am hungry, though. And tea and toast are probably about as brave as I should get for now. Is there jam, too?"

"No, but if you take the tray I'll go get you some."

"You don't have to."

"It's the least I can do since I made you sick with my cooking."

He'd made her sick all right, but not with his cooking alone. Of course, she couldn't say that, so instead she said, "That would be nice," even as she told herself she should have declined the offer, taken the tray and avoided spending any more time with him today.

But now that she felt good again she couldn't resist the opportunity to have more of what they'd been sharing in the kitchen when she'd gotten sick. Wise or not.

"I'll be back," Brady said, handing over the tray and turning on his heels to return to the kitchen.

Kate didn't mean to look at his derriere as he did, that just seemed to be where her gaze landed at that instant before she yanked her eyes off him and took the tray to the coffee table.

She set it down and then sat on the sofa, pouring the tea from a small silver pot into the china cup he'd brought, while still keeping an eye on the door. Not only was she eager to see him again but the moment he reappeared she said, "Would you close the door? I'm afraid of the bacon smell coming in here."

He did as she asked, then joined her on the couch. "You're making me feel guilty," he told her, referring to her most recent mention of the bacon.

"Good," she teased, not meaning it.

Brady leaned forward and put the strawberry jam on the toast for her.

"I think I can do that myself," she said with a laugh.

"Take advantage while you can," he advised.

She accepted the slice when he was finished with it and took a bite. "How did your rumaki go over with everyone else?" she asked then.

"Nobody but you ran out of the room with their hand over their mouth, so I guess it was a hit," he joked.

Kate held up the slice of bread to take another bite. "I can attest to your culinary skills with toast if that helps make up for my earlier insult to your talents."

"Makes me feel much better," he assured as they both settled back on the sofa, Kate with her tea and Brady sitting at enough of an angle to her to study her as if she were a sight for sore eyes.

Then, out of nowhere, he said, "You know I've been thinkin' that you never did tell me the details of that 'saving yourself for marriage' thing. How did you manage that? I mean, you're great looking. I would have thought there would have been a lot of hot pursuit of you that would have worn you down long before New Year's Eve."

"Hot pursuit of me?" she repeated with a laugh. "Hardly. I was a geek. Believe me, no one was in any kind of pursuit, hot or otherwise."

"I don't believe it."

"It's true. It took plastic surgery to have my ears pinned back to stop me from looking like Dumbo the Elephant Girl, and four years of braces on my teeth to correct nature's dastardly dentistry in my mouth."

"No," he said dubiously, looking more closely at her ears and then her teeth.

"I wouldn't lie about it. Didn't you notice what a

sight I was in those old photographs we put in the scrapbook the other night? I was a horrible geek until I was seventeen.''

"Okay, so you were a geek until you were seventeen. That still left a lot of years between then and New Year's Eve.''

"You're forgetting I also have four older brothers.''

"What did they do? Go out on your dates with you?''

"Dates? I didn't date. Nothing ever got that far. Even the few nerdy guys who showed the slightest bit of interest in me got chased off by my brothers before they so much as asked me out.''

"You didn't have a single date all through high school?" Brady recapped with disbelief.

"Not a single one. My brothers thought it was hilarious to scare off anybody who came within ten feet of me.''

"Big dumb jerks,'' he said affectionately.

"I called them a lot worse than that,'' Kate assured him. "But it never did any good.''

She'd finished her tea and toast so she set the cup on the coffee table and curled her feet up underneath her, pivoting slightly toward Brady to look at him while they talked.

There was a sense of closeness to sitting there like that with him and she was aware of just how nice it was. Not to mention that she was relishing the look in his eyes as he kept his gaze focused on her. A look of warmth. Of fondness. Of something more. Something that seemed very sensual.

And very dangerous because of the way it made her feel.

But she didn't want to analyze it. She didn't want to fight it. She just wanted to indulge in that sense she had that he found her so desirable he couldn't imagine that she'd ever been anything less to any other man.

"What about college?" he asked then. "You went away for that. There must have been guys who were after you on campus."

Kate held up two fingers. "It wasn't as if I'd developed great skills of flirtation," she admitted. "Or knew what to do with guys when they actually stuck around awhile and asked me out. I was awkward and, well, geeky, and after a couple of dates I never heard from either one of them again."

"And that was it? All through college you only went out a few times with two different guys?" Brady said, again as if he couldn't believe what he was hearing.

"That was it."

"What about after you graduated?"

That question took them to the present and to memories too painful for Kate to talk about as glibly as she'd told everything else.

Brady must have seen the change in her expression because he said, "Oh-oh. Here's where the inexperience hurts." He stretched an arm along the top of the sofa back behind her and squeezed her shoulder with one of those big hands.

It was a simple gesture of support, but just his touch was powerful enough to make Kate feel more than comforted. It also set off little sparks from that spot to rain all through her. Sparks that had absolutely nothing to do with comfort or compassion, and everything to do with bringing to life the kind of feelings he'd brought to life in Las Vegas. The kind of feelings that had made her throw caution to the wind.

Kate tried to ignore those feelings and said, "It wasn't the inexperience that hurt me. It was Dwight Mooney."

"He preyed on your innocence?" Brady guessed.

"No, in fact it was exactly what he was looking for, because he was just as inexperienced. By choice, though. His family was very old-fashioned and very religious. His father was a minister, in fact. They believed in not having sex out of marriage. Our both being virgins was a big deal to him."

Brady's eyebrows rose. "How long were you together?"

"Five years. After college I was busy concentrating on my career and still didn't date more than a couple of one-time deals. Then I met Dwight."

"You were together for five years and he never touched you?"

Kate had to smile at the complete shock in Brady's tone. "He kissed me," she offered.

"But that's all?"

"That's all."

"Wow."

"I know, it sounds pretty extreme. But that's what he was committed to, and I thought the ability to make such a strong commitment to something—especially something as tough as that—was a good sign. A sign of character. And since we got engaged a year into the relationship, I honestly thought that anytime we'd be getting married and the wait would be over."

"And even once you were engaged? Nothing?"

"Kissing. Only kissing. Anything else was against his religion."

"Were you okay with that?"

Kate thought about it. "Well, I don't know. I didn't expect the engagement to go on for so long, that's for sure. He kept putting off setting a date and I didn't like that. But I thought Dwight was a good man. He treated me well. He was attentive. Caring. He said we were building a foundation to base our life together on, and I hoped that was true. I hoped his passion for his religion and his commitments would translate into passion for me once we were married and he felt free to…consummate it."

"Okay, I guess I can see that," Brady conceded.

"Plus, I loved him and I felt as comfortable with Dwight as I did with my brothers. I thought that meant I had found my other half, the man I was meant to be with. And the fact that he was someone who wouldn't expect me to…know what I was doing in the bedroom made the whole thing seem like he was the guy for me.''

Brady's face creased into a pained kind of smile, and he dropped his head to the top of hers. ''Oh, Kate,'' he said, sighing her name into her hair. Then he raised his head again and said, ''I'd like to take all four of those brothers of yours, hog-tie 'em and hang 'em by their heels in the hot sun.''

Kate laughed. ''Why?''

''Because their foolin' around made you think you had to settle for a guy who could keep his hands off you for five years.''

She hadn't thought of it like that.

''Tell me you finally saw there was somethin' wrong with good ol' Dwight and gave him the heave-ho.''

''I'd like to tell you that, but it wouldn't be the truth,'' she said softly, because in spite of Brady's more flattering perspective, Dwight had hurt her deeply.

''What happened?'' Brady asked kindly.

Kate took a deep breath to shore up for telling what she hadn't admitted to many people since it had happened. ''I thought we were on the verge of finally setting a date for the wedding. I'd even told my friend Kelly to keep April—next month—open so we could have a spring wedding. I was all ready to start picking out bridesmaids' dresses and flowers and a caterer—'' An unexpected catch in Kate's voice stalled her a moment while she tamped down the pain, rejection and humiliation she'd thought she'd put behind her.

"The idiot broke it off with you?" Brady asked with another full measure of disbelief that helped bolster her.

"Worse," she said. "Dwight eloped with a woman who lived in the apartment across the hall from me. She was a stripper who ran so many men in and out of her place that Dwight and I had wondered if she was—"

"Playing for pay?" Brady supplied.

"Yes." She took another deep breath and consciously attempted to sigh away the bad feelings the subject had raised.

"How did Dwight get from saint to sinner so fast?"

"He moved her couch one night."

Brady laughed, picking up on the levity she was trying to inject into this subject that was so difficult for her.

"He moved her couch," he repeated. "That'll do it every time."

"They had come up on the elevator together one night, and when she recognized him from seeing him going in and out of my place she asked if he'd help her out. He told me afterward that he'd only agreed because it was the Christian thing to do."

"Right," Brady said facetiously.

"Anyway, I didn't think anything about it. After all, he was so good at resisting me, it didn't occur to me that he'd have any problem resisting anyone else. Especially someone he'd talked about with such scorn before that.''

"What was he doing, just covering up the hots for her all along?"

"According to his explanation on the phone from Reno, the couch moving had only been the beginning of something between them that he *couldn't* resist. They'd been seeing each other on the sly since then, and he'd discovered a drive in himself that he hadn't known he'd had when he was with me. He said it was just something he couldn't do anything about, and since he still didn't want to act on it outside of marriage—''

"He eloped with her."

"He eloped with her."

Brady closed his eyes in a tight grimace and shook his head. "Incredible."

Then he opened his eyes again to look at her with that penetrating blue gaze. "And that was why you were more than ready to shed your virginity a little over a month later in Las Vegas," he concluded.

"Sort of," she agreed.

"But not really?"

"There was just a lot more to what happened in Las Vegas than that."

"Shall I guess? Dwight's elopement was all it took to make you feel the way you had before meeting him—undesirable, unappealing, not pretty enough. And a little fling was a good ego booster."

"Yes," she admitted tentatively, amazed that he understood her so well. "But that wasn't all there was to it, either," she added then, not wanting him to think what she was afraid he thought. Especially when it wasn't true. "I wasn't using you."

He laughed lightly at that. "Ah, Kate. There's nobody quite like you. I never thought you were using me."

"I mean, you were so much fun to be with and I was having such a good time—" She'd almost said she'd also been so attracted to him that she just hadn't been able to help herself, but stopped short of that. Instead she said, "I just got carried away by it all. Losing my virginity... Well, yes, I was ready to do that, but it wasn't as if I'd planned to do it. It was actually the last thing on my mind until... Until things started happening between us."

Brady put a knuckle to her chin to make her look directly at him. "I *was* fun to be with and you *were* having a good time? All past tense?" he said, his tone teasing but edged with a note of seriousness, too, as if he were concerned she might be telling him things had changed now and she wasn't enjoying his company.

"We were talking about the past, weren't we?" she reminded him, rather than expose just how much she did like being with him.

"Okay, then what about now?" he persisted with a half grin that was pure devil, the kind Dwight would never have known how to give.

And Kate basked in it.

"Now you're making me sick," she teased, referring to the bacon incident.

But Brady missed the reference and went on the alert. "Right this minute? Again?"

Kate laughed. "I was talking about this afternoon. I feel great now." More than great. She felt warm and comfortable and relaxed and alive all at once. And very aware of those sparks that he'd ignited in her, still dancing through her veins as if they were electrical wires.

Brady's expression eased and he smiled again. Slowly this time, with those eyes so bright they made her heart ache.

"You *look* great," he said with so much of what sounded like genuine appreciation that Kate believed him in a way she'd never believed it before. "But tell me that you're still having fun with me," he ordered, not letting her off the hook that easily.

"Okay, okay, I'm still having fun with you," she finally admitted.

It pleased him because his smile turned into a grin. A grin she got lost in.

"Now tell me you don't hate it that I'm hanging around so much."

"I don't hate it that you're hanging around so much."

"And I'm not forcin' myself on you?"

She laughed. "Forcing yourself on me?"

"When you'd rather be readin' a book or somethin'."

"I haven't felt forced upon, no."

Her responses—even though they were prompted—seemed to please him because his grin reappeared moments before he kissed her.

His knuckle at her chin somehow became his hand caressing her jaw and the side of her face to guide her as his mouth came over hers in a soft kiss. But soft or not, after having talked about Dwight, Kate couldn't help comparing even that fledgling kiss to kisses her ex-fiancé had given. No wonder they had the power to do so much to her, she thought, because even that tender, beginning buss was so much better, so much more intriguing, so much more potent than anything Dwight had ever bestowed.

And when Brady deepened the kiss, when his lips parted and urged hers to part, too, when his tongue came to say hello, he left Dwight in the dust. In fact, he wiped Dwight right out of her mind as his arms came around her and pulled her up against him, his hands massaging her back through the velvety fleece of her jumpsuit.

Between his kiss and his touch those sparks dancing along her veins turned into little flames that made her answer his teasing tongue thrust for thrust, taunt for taunt. They brought her arms around him, too, and inspired her hands to fill themselves with the hard expanse of his back, with the roll of honed muscles and the breadth of shoulders strong enough to bear the weight of the world.

Her breasts were pressed to his chest, yearning, striving for attention. For the kind of attention that Kate barely remembered from Las Vegas and yet craved with a sudden intensity that nearly drove her wild. Wild enough to arch her back, to press them more insistently into the wall of a man that was Brady.

Oh, how she wanted him to touch her!

Just then one wonderful hand began a slow slide from her back to her side, slower still to the straining globe of her breast until he cupped it in his big palm.

A small moan of pleasure escaped her throat with that initial contact, and she instantly wished the jumpsuit would disappear so she could feel the full impact of his skin against hers.

Their mouths were open wide by then in a seeking, hungering kiss that gave Kate the courage to slip her own hands under the knit of his Henley shirt to his bare back. Hot satin over steel—that was what it felt like—and she couldn't get enough of it, digging her fingertips into taut sinew in a way that unconsciously mimicked the kneading her breasts were crying out for. So much so that her spine had arched even more, insinuating that single globe firmly into his adept hand.

He seemed to be perfectly in tune with her, with her needs, because just when she thought she couldn't endure a moment more of the barrier of cloth, he deserted her breast altogether so he could pull the zipper of her jumpsuit down. Inch by snail's-crawl inch until it was finally low enough for him to give her what she wanted, what she needed, so desperately—her bare breast engulfed in his bare hand.

Another groan echoed in her throat as bliss washed through her with such force she nearly felt faint.

She'd realized that pregnancy had made her breasts more sensitive, but she hadn't known there would be so much more pleasure in that sensitivity until that moment when nothing came between his kneading, teasing, seeking hand and her oh-so-aroused flesh.

In fact, the pleasure was so great, so intense, it tore her mouth from his kiss as she nearly writhed beneath the exquisite things he was doing to her. Her nipple kerneled into a tight knot in his palm. A knot he rolled gently between his fingers, traced round and round, and tormented so deliciously she almost couldn't contain herself as everything inside her came awake with a jolt of need, of wanting, of desire for even more of what he was doing to her. For his mouth to be where his hand was. For his hand to be lower still. For more than his hand to find that place between her legs that was thrumming to life....

But that was when he stopped. Suddenly. As if something had just occurred to him.

Just when she wanted so much more, his glorious hand slipped completely out of her jumpsuit, zipping it up to her throat.

"Brady?" she said in a husky whisper that sounded more vulnerable than she wished it had.

He kissed her again, but only softly, quickly, before he laid his cheek to hers for a moment and then sat back.

"I don't think we better push this after your being so sick this afternoon," he said in a voice as raspy as hers had been.

"I'm fine. Really," she heard herself say before

thinking better of it, before realizing how much of her own need it revealed.

But even that didn't matter.

"Fine is how I want you to stay feeling, too," he said with a conviction that sounded as if it were warring with a hunger as strong in him as the hunger that was still coursing through her.

And yet, despite that hunger, there was something else in his expression that kept her from saying more. Something in his eyes. A look she couldn't read.

But what popped into her mind after a split second was the thought that somewhere in the middle of things he'd figured he wasn't going to make the same mistake he'd made in Las Vegas no matter what raw desire might be urging him to.

And that stabbed her as surely as any knife might have, even as a part of her was still wishing he would pick up where he'd left off.

But he didn't take her into his arms the way she wanted him to. He didn't kiss her again or touch her. He certainly didn't carry her off to bed to make love to her.

Instead he stood and said, "Get some rest."

It was on the tip of her tongue to say she'd just had a nap. But she didn't. If he didn't want her, he didn't want her, and nothing she said could change that—she knew it only too well after her experience with Dwight.

"If you get sick during the night and need me—need anything at all—just holler," he said then.

"I'll be fine," she told him stiffly but very, very quietly as old feelings of rejection set in.

He stood there staring at her, frowning, searching for something she couldn't fathom. But he wasn't about to let her in on it because he just said, "Sleep tight then," and turned on his heels to go out of the room on long strides that seemed to pound thorns into her heart with every step he took away from her.

Then he was out the door, closing it behind him, and Kate was left even more confused than she'd been before.

Confused and hurt and wanting him so much it was an empty ache inside her.

Chapter Ten

Kate was just getting over the next day's morning sickness when she had a phone call. She took it in her bedroom with the door closed, because she had a good idea who her caller was even before she picked up. She also had a good idea what they'd be talking about.

Kate's best friend, Kelly McGill, had been scheduled to return from her vacation in Mexico late the previous night, and Kate was expecting to hear from her.

Sure enough, the voice on the other end of the line that answered Kate's hello belonged to Kelly.

"Well?" was all Kelly said.

Kate didn't need any more explanation than that.

She knew Kelly wanted to know if the doctor in Cheyenne had confirmed that Kate was pregnant.

"Yes," Kate answered in a quiet voice.

"You're pregnant," Kelly said with a sigh.

"Yes."

"Shall I say congratulations or I'm sorry?"

Kate laughed a little at that. "Congratulations. I think."

"Okay. Congratulations. And whatever you do, don't marry the father."

Kate laughed again, understanding perfectly her friend's comment. "Speaking of Buster..." she said. "How did he do with the boys while you were gone?"

"About the usual. Not well. They were happy to see me and glad to leave him, and he made it clear he was just as glad to have them go."

It was Kate's turn to sigh. "I keep hoping he'll finally step up to the plate, but he just doesn't, does he?"

"No. And if he hasn't by now, he never will. He's out of work again, too, by the way."

"Not again."

"And, as always, according to him it's my fault."

"Same old song and dance?"

"Yes. If I hadn't gotten pregnant and he hadn't had to marry me he'd have finished college the way he'd planned and now he wouldn't be getting passed over for promotions in favor of people with degrees."

"I suppose it's also your fault that he mouths off or storms out of his jobs on a whim."

"Of course. I'm responsible for ruining his life and that's why he has a bad attitude—that's what he tells me every time. As if I was alone in that back seat that night or planned to get pregnant. Like I said, don't marry the father, whatever you do. It's better for you and the baby to avoid this kind of resentment. Before and after the inevitable divorce that comes out of some guy marrying you because he thinks he has to."

Kelly said that matter-of-factly and with a minimum of bitterness because Buster's resentment was a plain fact she'd been living with for so long now. A plain fact Kate didn't want to experience for herself.

"Believe me, I don't have any intention of marrying anybody," Kate told her friend, feeling a renewed conviction that came with the reminder of how even what had begun as a loving relationship could deteriorate so disastrously.

"Is the dad there at the ranch?" Kelly asked then.

Kate had told her originally that Brady was due for a visit within days of her doctor's appointment.

"Right in the room beside mine. And he's buying the place next door, too."

"You'll be neighbors. Is that good or bad?" Kelly asked in the same tone she'd used to inquire if she should offer congratulations or sympathies on the pregnancy.

"I don't know yet," Kate said honestly.

"You haven't let him know you're pregnant?"

"I haven't let anybody but you know I'm pregnant—well, you and Junebug. But she guessed. I haven't told my family or Brady, either."

"I know you'll tell your family eventually. But are you going to tell Brady?"

"I don't think there's any way around it, do you?"

"And depending on his reaction, it could be good that he'll be close by to actually be a father to the baby or bad if he acts like Buster does."

"That's about it," Kate confirmed, not adding that it could also be bad to have Brady so nearby, where she would have to watch him go on with his life— his life with other women—and how painful that might be for her.

But Kelly knew her too well. "What about your feelings for him?" she said as if she were privy to Kate's thoughts. "You really liked the guy in Las Vegas. He's been almost all you've talked about ever since."

"I haven't been that bad. Have I?"

"Pretty much. We haven't had a single conversation that you haven't brought him up one way or another."

Kate knew Brady had been on her mind almost nonstop since January, but she hadn't realized she'd talked about him that much. She wasn't heartened to be made aware of it now. "He's a nice enough guy," she hedged.

"You're liking him more and more, aren't you?" Kelly said, again reading Kate like a book.

"I'm trying not to," Kate confessed.

"Oh, Kate," Kelly said as if she'd just heard something that scared her.

"I won't do anything dumb," Kate said firmly. "But it would be better for everybody if we had a civil relationship."

"Civil, yes. But don't forget you have happy hormones at work. Nature designed them to make you look at the father of your baby and think he's a prince whether he is or not. Keep that in mind."

"You weren't thinking Buster was a prince when he didn't show up in the delivery room because he was playing softball and wouldn't leave."

"I'm just saying—"

"I know. It's easy to want to believe in the happily ever after fairy tale."

Kelly didn't say anything for a moment. Then she switched gears. "Of course, just because things didn't work out for me, doesn't mean they won't work out for you. Maybe this Brady guy *is* a prince. Maybe he's always wanted a family and he fell in love with you at first sight in Las Vegas and he'll be thrilled to his toes to find out he can have the whole package all at once."

"He is a nice guy. But he's already said he isn't ready for a family yet."

"You were fishing?"

"Maybe a little. Just to get a feel for how he might react when I tell him. And believe me, I'm the last person on earth with any illusions about my being such an irresistible force that he'll change his mind on the spot.''

''Just because you weren't an irresistible force to Dwight doesn't mean you won't be to someone else.''

Kate laughed. ''How many pregnant irresistible forces do you know?''

''Don't get down on yourself, Kate. You're great, pregnant or not pregnant. Dwight was just an idiot.''

''That's me all right...great,'' Kate said with false bravado.

''So when are you going to tell him?''

Kate explained her decision to wait until the divorce papers were filed so it would be clear she didn't want to stay married to him.

But even as she was saying the words, she was thinking that, when she did finally tell him about the baby, everything would change. That what had begun to happen between them in these last few days and nights would end. And so would the way he made her feel—attractive, desirable, sexy, irresistible....

Maybe what was going through her mind echoed in her tone because when she was finished Kelly said, ''Are you going to be okay?''

''Sure,'' Kate said with more confidence than she felt.

''Why don't you duck out and come here to stay with the boys and me for a while? To get away.''

''Thanks but I'd kind of like to wait things out here so as soon as I know the divorce is final I can tell him and get it over with.''

But that was a lie. The truth was that being presented with an option to put some real distance between herself and Brady only pushed Kate to realize she didn't want to be too far from him. From all those things he was making her feel.

"Well, if you won't come to stay you can at least call and talk through what you're going to say to him beforehand. Practice on me," Kelly offered.

Kate laughed again. "I might do that. Dress rehearsal."

"But if you don't you'll let me know when you do tell him?"

"You know I will."

"And you also know I'm here for you, don't you?"

"You always have been." Sounds of angry voices had been coming from the background on Kelly's end of the line for several minutes, and they seemed to have gained heat and volume suddenly. "Are the boys fighting?"

"I think they're trying to kill each other."

"You better go break it up before they do."

"I know. I'm just worried about you."

"I'll be fine," Kate assured. "Go take care of your kids."

"We'll talk soon."

"Soon," Kate confirmed before they said their goodbyes and hung up.

"Oh, man, is it beautiful up here! I don't know why you got the bug to take me flyin' today, but what a day for it—not a cloud in the sky, the trees just beginnin' to bud, fresh snow in the high country—incredible! And worth all those peeved looks we got when we said we were duckin' out for an hour while everybody else gets things ready for Buzz's party tonight.''

Brady smiled at Matt's enthusiasm, barely noticing the splendor his friend was talking about as Brady piloted his plane to the farthest reaches of the McDermot property and beyond.

The view wasn't the reason Brady wanted to get Matt up there. His real purpose was to get away from Kate. Only this time, he wanted to get away from Kate not because of the hot, simmering attraction he had for her. This time he just wanted to make absolutely sure she didn't overhear what he needed to ask her brother. He wanted to make sure no one overheard it.

''You don't look like you're enjoyin' this as much as I am, though,'' Matt said then. ''In fact, you look like you've been up all night and could use some sleep.''

''A touch of insomnia last night,'' Brady said as if it were nothing, when in fact he hadn't been able to sleep for good reason. He'd been up pacing the floor, thinking things he was determined to have confirmed or refuted this morning.

But not in any forthright way. So, as if he were merely changing the subject because his sleeplessness was too negligible to discuss, he said, ''How's Kate been since Las Vegas?''

"What're you doin'? Lookin' to find out if she missed you?"

"No, it's just that she finally told me about that Dwight guy and how she was comin' off his eloping with someone else when we met. I wondered if Las Vegas helped and she was back to her old self afterward."

Matt gave him a sly smile. "Or maybe what you're really wonderin' is if she might be ready to move on to a new relationship now," he said, gloating over what he was apparently choosing to believe was his successful matchmaking.

"Has she been seein' anybody?"

Again Matt interpreted that to suit himself and his own goals. "No, you've got a clear field there. She's about been hibernating. Has hardly left the ranch except to get things goin' for her office. Been doin' a lot of sleepin'."

"She hasn't dated anyone at all?"

"Not a soul. At least not anybody around Elk Creek."

"But how about outside of Elk Creek? Any trips anywhere else? Somewhere she might have hooked up with somebody?" Brady asked.

Matt turned his head to look straight at Brady. "I can't believe how off your game you are since Claudia left you. What are you? Scared of competition? That isn't like you."

"I'm just thinkin' that Kate could have something goin' on with somebody outside of Elk Creek."

"She hasn't taken any trips anywhere. I told you,

she hasn't left the ranch except to go into town, now and then. The truth is, we've been figurin' she's still mendin' a broken heart over Dwight. She's seemed kind of under the weather. She's pale. Not a lot of energy. Not eatin' much. And like I said, sleepin' way more than any of us have ever known her to sleep. She was perky enough in Vegas, but it didn't carry over once we got her back here.'' Matt grinned slyly as he added, ''Maybe it's just you who makes her feel better.''

Brady ignored the comment. ''So she was the same before Vegas—sleepin' a lot, not eatin', under the weather? Vegas was a change of pace for her and then she went right back to it?''

Matt thought about that. Then he said, ''Now that you mention it, no, she wasn't doin' that stuff before. She was unhappy. Real down in the dumps. But she was eatin' fine. And *not* bein' able to sleep was more her problem then. She was stayin' up later than anybody every night and out in the kitchen in the mornings before us all. It's only been lately...''

Matt did a mock glare in response to his own words sinking in. ''Hey, did you do somethin' to my sister in Las Vegas that made her worse off?'' he joked.

Unfortunately there was nothing funny to Brady in that possibility. Still, he didn't want to raise his friend's curiosity or suspicions so he said, ''Nah. We had a good time in Vegas. You just said yourself she was in a better mood when we were there. Maybe she just got away from her troubles for that time and then got the blues all over again when she got back.''

"Yeah, that makes sense," Matt agreed.

"I'm not sure what you're talkin' about when you say she looks pale, though," Brady said to segue into the other questions he had. "In fact, I was wonderin' if she might've done something to herself."

"Done something to herself?" Matt repeated. "What do you mean? Like new makeup or hair or something?"

"Yeah. Or even like plastic surgery."

Matt cast him a glance that said he thought Brady was crazy. "Plastic surgery? As in a nose job or somethin'?"

Actually what Brady was thinking about was south of her nose. Pretty far south.

"It's not her nose, no. I just thought there was something a little different about her," Brady persisted.

"Nah, she didn't have plastic surgery," Matt continued. "I told you, she's been at the ranch the whole time since Vegas." Then Matt laughed. "Oh, I get it. She's lookin' even better to you now than she did New Year's and you're tryin' to figure out why."

It wasn't so much the way she looked as the way she felt. But Brady couldn't say that to her brother.

Matt chuckled again with obvious pleasure. "Things startin' up with you two, are they? No wonder you've spent more time with her than with me since you got here."

Brady forced a smile that seemed to confirm that,

all the while thinking that he was afraid something might have started up with Kate but not what Matt was figuring on.

"Hey, who is it who's been busy with a woman?" Brady countered.

Matt grinned. "Yeah, I know. I spend every minute I can with Jenn. I wasn't complainin' about you bein' with Kate. My findin' Jenn was the best thing that ever happened to me. I can't tell you how I feel about her. One look at her face and I just fill up inside. Makes me want that for everybody. Especially for my best friend and my sister."

"How about working out?" Brady said when another possibility occurred to him in the middle of what Matt had been saying. "Has Kate been exercising or lifting weights to…you know…build herself up or something?"

"Working out? No, she hasn't been working out. Like I said, she's been sleepin' till nearly noon every day. Says she's takin' advantage of her time off while she has it." Matt poked him in the ribs with an elbow. "She's *really* lookin' good to you, huh?"

"Yeah," Brady admitted truthfully. "She's really looking good to me."

"And how's she actin'?"

"How's she acting?" Brady repeated.

"Did you take my advice and get her to open up to you? Get things rollin' so she'd develop an interest in you?"

An interest in him? Brady supposed it could be called that. But he had to hope there was more to it than simple interest. Especially after the previous night when she'd just about driven him wild with wanting her. So wild that he'd been headed for making love to her again until it struck him that something was different about her. About her body. And even though he'd tried to write it off to his memories of New Year's Eve being too foggy to be reliable, the more he'd touched her, the more he'd begun to believe that his memories might be more reliable than he thought....

"I can't be sure what's going on with her," Brady said, belatedly answering Matt's question about whether or not Kate was interested in him.

"Is she still keepin' you at arm's length?"

Brady could hardly tell his friend that Kate had let him get a whole lot closer than that, so instead he said, "We've both just learned to be cautious."

"I think you both just worry too much."

"Maybe," Brady agreed, all the while thinking that he just might have more to worry about than Matt realized.

Maybe a whole lot more....

Chapter Eleven

Kate chose her favorite dress for her grandfather's birthday party that evening. She'd tried it on a few days earlier, and although it still fit, she knew it was likely to be the last time she could wear it until after the baby was born. It was an ankle-length cashmere tube the soft-brown color of milk chocolate. And while it wasn't formfitting, it didn't have much room to spare.

She showered late in the day and washed her hair, leaving it to air dry with a few finger-scrunchings along the way to ensure that it curled enough to wear loose, and with the hour the guests were to arrive fast approaching, she slipped the dress on over her string-bikini panties and bandeau bra.

The bandeau bra was a necessity because the dress

had a wide boat neck that would expose straps. But she loved the three-inch V-split the neckline took in the center at the base of her throat so it was worth the slight sense of insecurity to go without straps.

The sleeves were three-quarter length, freeing her wrists for the dozen small beaded bracelets she and Maya had each bought on a whim in town the week before.

A little blush and mascara were the only dabs of makeup she applied. Then she combed her hair into a wild array of curls that ended in a blunt-cut at her jaw. She slipped her feet into a pair of thin-heeled strappy pumps and took a close look at the finished product in the full-length mirror, turning to the side for the most important view.

The increase in her bust size caused the cashmere to fall far enough away from the slight bulge of her belly so that her pregnancy was hardly noticeable at all. She could rest assured that no one was likely to guess at her condition.

"But even if they do, it's okay," she reminded herself.

It was okay because she'd already made up her mind that she was going to tell Brady about the baby very soon, whether the divorce papers were filed or not. She'd decided that signing them was message enough of her intentions and that she would reinforce that when she told him by insisting the divorce still be finalized. But in the meantime, she'd be taking some action. Before it was too late.

Her talk with Kelly had brought her to the conclusion that it was best not to keep the secret any longer. What had happened with Brady the night before had been on her mind, and realizing she was dragging her feet about getting away from him when she'd spoken to Kelly had set off warning bells inside her. The conversation had left her knowing more than ever that she was playing with fire to let things go on the way they had been.

It wasn't a matter of just forming a friendship or a civil relationship on which to base their co-parenting, the way she'd tried to convince herself it was. Friends didn't keep ending up in each other's arms. They didn't keep ending up kissing each other. Touching each other. Very nearly making love to each other. And she had to stop fooling herself that friendship or mere civility was all there was to it.

At least for her.

She couldn't be sure what was happening on Brady's side. But she had to face the fact that she was getting in over her head.

"As if having his baby doesn't already count as getting in over my head," she muttered in response to her own thoughts as she applied a light lip gloss.

But still, she knew that the feelings that were coming to life inside her just as surely as the baby itself was, were only compounding her problems. The plain truth was that no matter what she'd told herself along the way, and no matter how dangerous she knew it was, she was coming to care for Brady.

Maybe Kelly was right and it was those happy hormones her friend had talked about, but she just couldn't let what had gone on so far keep going on. Keep progressing. And since her willpower was nearly nonexistent when it came to Brady, she'd decided that the best thing to do was to drop the bomb she believed would change everything for her whether she liked it or not. And put an end to what needed to be ended.

Before it was too late and her feelings for him got any stronger.

Before it was too late and Brady looked back on everything that had happened between them since he'd arrived at the ranch and wondered if it had all been devised to trap him.

So she was going to tell him. At the first possible moment.

And maybe then things would be put on the straight and narrow where they should have been all along.

And hopefully it wouldn't hurt too much.

Since Buzz had been born, raised and had lived his whole life in Elk Creek, the party to celebrate his eightieth birthday was a big one. His only daughter— Kate, Ry, Shane, Bax and Matt's mother—had intended to be there but had been kept away by a case of bronchitis that had prohibited her from flying in. She was hardly missed, though. With so many of the townsfolk there it seemed as if the entire citizenry had come to pay homage to the elderly man who held court in the living room.

Kate and the rest of the McDermot women, along

with Junebug, were kept busy seeing to the needs
and comfort of their guests, so it should have been
easy for Kate to have been completely oblivious of
Brady. To not even notice him.

But that wasn't the case.

All of her brothers put effort into introducing him
around, making sure every person there met him and
learned he'd just bought the Barton place and would
be a member of the community. But somehow those
introductions never took place far from where Kate
was. And even as Brady engaged in conversation that
she could tell was already making him well liked,
each time Kate glanced up she found his gaze
crossing to her as if he were still more aware of her
than of anyone else in the house.

Of course, despite the crowd and her own chats
with everyone, Kate was still more aware of Brady
than of anyone else in the house, too. It was just
impossible for her not to be.

This realization really didn't make sense to her,
but like the previous day in her office—when it had
occurred to her that the sight of Jace Brimley didn't
have the same effect on her that the sight of Brady
did, even standing in the midst of five of Junebug's
six strikingly handsome sons—it was still Brady who
caught Kate's eye.

He wasn't any taller than the Brimley men. Or
broader of shoulder or narrower of hip. His dark,
longish hair wasn't any more remarkable, and while
there was no disputing his drop-dead good looks,
Junebug's sons were like a gallery of gorgeous men

all standing around in a circle. And yet not one of them riveted Kate's attention the way Brady did.

Happy hormones, she told herself. That's all it was.

But whether or not that was true, nothing changed the fact that she was attuned to his every movement. That she devoured the sight of his thick thighs and tight derriere in the black jeans he wore. That she feasted on the sight of him in the dove-gray Western shirt that hugged his waist, while his mile-wide shoulders were saddle-bagged in a black design that came to points over pectorals she wanted stripped bare before her so she could run her hands over the honed chest muscles.

And try as she might she just couldn't seem to stay distracted from him even at a distance. As far as she was concerned they might as well have been alone in the house, even though they rarely got near enough to speak.

At the first sign that the guests were beginning to leave, Junebug started a surreptitious cleanup so that by midnight, when the last of them were gone and Buzz had taken himself off to bed, there wasn't anything left to do that couldn't wait for the morning.

"Just let the rest be, until tomorrow," the imposing housekeeper instructed as she put on her coat and headed for home with her family in tow.

No one seemed inclined to go against the housekeeper's wishes and instead good-nights were in the process of being said as Kate bent over to remove her shoes, because she didn't think she could stand them long enough to walk to her room.

But when she straightened up it was to find herself alone in the kitchen with Brady as everyone else wandered off to their rooms.

He was watching her with the same quiet study that had been in his blue-gray eyes all evening, and it was beginning to make her wonder what he was thinking about to put it there.

But he didn't give her any clue when he said, "Nice party."

"I hope everyone thought so," she responded, as the deep rye whisky of his voice seemed to wash her in warmth for no reason she could put her finger on.

"You know what I didn't get, though?"

She knew what she hadn't gotten—time with him to appease the unwanted craving for it.

But all she said was, "What?"

"Birthday cake. How about it? Are you up for a birthday cake nightcap?"

There it was—the perfect opportunity to sit down with him and tell him she was pregnant.

But now that the moment had presented itself, Kate hesitated.

It was very late. She was tired. Wouldn't it be better to wait until tomorrow, when she was rested and so was he? When it didn't come as some sort of afterthought?

Okay, so maybe she was only hedging. But what harm would a few more hours' postponement do?

"Birthday cake sounds good," she heard herself

say, even as a voice in the back of her mind was warning her she was playing with fire yet again.

"I'll tell you what, you've worked all day, so you go to your room where you can be comfortable, and I'll serve you for a change."

Kate figured her fatigue was showing, and in truth she really was too tired to fight a suggestion that was so appealing. So she said, "Just a little piece of cake for me," and did as she'd been told.

She'd hardly had a chance to drop her shoes, sit on the sofa in her sitting room and put her feet up when Brady followed, carrying two plates.

He handed her one and then pointed a finger of his free hand at his boots. "Do you mind?"

Kate shook her head, and off came his cowboy boots before he joined her on the couch and propped his feet beside hers.

A flood of emotion welled up in her at the intimacy of his two big feet so casually next to her much smaller ones, and she tried to fight her reaction. But there was something about him being in his stocking feet that just made her feel that way.

I must really be tired if something that inconsequential can move me, she thought.

"Good cake," Brady observed then, after his second bite.

Kate forced herself to concentrate on that, rather than on their feet, and tasted it herself.

"But no ice cream," she countered once she had.

"We already ate our share of that, remember? That was the deal—we had ours so we couldn't eat any tonight.'' Then he gave her a half grin. ''Besides, I looked and it was all gone.''

Kate didn't want to like him as much as she did at that moment, but she couldn't help that, either. Although, in an attempt to keep her perspective she did force herself to say, ''Have you sent the divorce papers to the lawyer yet?''

That sobered Brady somewhat. ''Not yet,'' he said. Then he added, ''I'm sorry, but I think there's a law against talkin' about stuff like that while eatin' cake this good. And I'll have to enforce it.''

''Ah,'' she said with a slight laugh.

They ate in silence for a little while. Brady seemed somewhat lost in thought, and Kate had the oddest sense that he might be trying to tell *her* something.

Or maybe she was just projecting her own thoughts on to him. But somehow, coupled with the abrupt ending of what had been happening between them the previous night, she was slightly unnerved by the possibility that he might actually be looking for the right moment to say his piece. Maybe to say that he really had stopped short because he felt it would have been a mistake to go any further. That he was uncomfortable with the directions things had taken with them again....

But just as Kate's fears mounted Brady said, ''No sickness tonight?''

There wasn't anything in his tone to lead her to think he had anything else on his mind, and she relaxed a little. ''You mean like last night?'' she asked for the sake of clarification.

"Mmm," he confirmed as he took another bite of cake.

"No flu tonight," she said honestly, setting her plate on the coffee table because she'd had enough.

Brady finished his slice and then hers, too, without any indication that what she'd been worried might be going through his head was a reality.

Then he proved he wasn't thinking about telling her he was uncomfortable with the direction things had taken with them because once he'd leaned forward to pile the dishes together on the coffee table he hooked his arm around her legs and brought them with him as he sat back, swiveling her so that she was sideways on the sofa with her legs across his lap. And the intimacy of their feet together on the coffee table was nothing compared to that.

"I didn't get a chance to tell you how great you look tonight," he said as he angled himself to get a more direct view of her, settling in to massage her calves and ankles with a familiarity that only increased the sense of intimacy.

"Thank you," she said in a breathier voice than she'd intended as his hands set glittering things to light inside her.

"I kept trying to get close enough to tell you that earlier, but every time I headed in your direction you seemed to go the other way."

"Not on purpose," she said. "I was just busy playing hostess."

The man should have been a masseur, Kate

thought as he continued working on her legs, chasing away the weariness in them.

"I thought maybe you were steerin' clear of me because of last night."

"You were the one who seemed to want space last night," she reminded.

"Space? Was that what I wanted last night?" he said with a sly smile.

"That's how it seemed. I thought it was the logical conclusion when you left in such a hurry."

He gave her a devil's grin. "Logical? There wasn't anything logical about last night."

"What was it then?" she challenged, as his hands around her ankles did wicked things to those glitters, sending them into a wild dance.

"Last night was crazy and overpowering and... great. It was great."

"So great you had to stop as if you'd been burned and were running for your life."

"Oh, are you wrong," he said with a chuckle and a shake of his head.

"Explain it then."

"Let's just say it had to do with how good you felt to me and with things that were goin' through my head."

He raised one of her legs enough to press a light kiss where her ankle curved into her foot.

Tell him now and get it over with, a little voice in the back of her mind recommended. *Tell him now and stop this before it goes any further....*

But already those glittery things he'd set to life

were burning brighter, turning to sparks, and she knew she wasn't going to do any such thing. Not right then. Not when it *would* end things....

"Why do we keep circlin' around each other, Kate?" he asked then, running his thumbs up her shinbones in a stroke that made her pulse pick up speed. "We keep goin' round and round, like two scared foals, comin' together in the center to bump noses but always backin' up again to circle each other some more."

"I don't know about you but I'm just sitting here," she joked in a voice more breathy still.

He took hold of her legs and pulled her nearer, so that she was sitting with her rear end against one of his thighs. Then, at that closer range, he looked into her eyes with a piercing intensity.

"I don't want you to be scared of me, Kate."

"I'm not scared of you."

"Yes, you are. But you don't need to be. I won't hurt you. I won't hurt you," he repeated with emphasis on each word as if to make what he was saying sink in.

But she knew better. She knew he'd already made her want things that would never be and not having them would hurt.

"Trust me," he commanded in a near whisper of a voice that beckoned, too.

Then, while one hand stayed resting on her knee, the other came to the back of her head to bring her to the kiss he pressed to her lips. Softly. Sweetly. A kiss that added to the enticement of his words, his voice.

And somehow Kate knew that tonight he would go through with what he'd so prematurely ended the evening before. That if she didn't stop him now, he wouldn't stop himself. He'd make love to her.

But should she let him? Should she go through with it knowing what she knew?

Then it occurred to her that maybe she should go through with it *because* she knew what she knew. *Because* she knew that once he found out she was pregnant things would take a different turn. And that when they did she wouldn't have this chance again. The chance to have his hands on her the way they had been in Las Vegas. To have him wrapped around her, every part of their bodies entwined and touching. The chance to have him make love to her just one more time before she put everything else in motion.

Still, she probably shouldn't let anything happen, she told herself.

But her thoughts didn't have much impact. Because no matter what lay ahead, no matter what happened or what he might end up thinking, she wanted this single night, she wanted him too much to deny herself.

So she would trust him. She would trust him not to hold it against her when he found out she'd known she was pregnant and kept it a secret while indulging in this time with him. She would trust him not to think it had been any kind of trap. To believe that it was what it was—a deep desire, a deep need, just to connect with him on a much more intimate level than their bare feet sharing the same coffee table or her legs crossed over his. On the most intimate of all levels. To have him want her so much that he couldn't resist her any more than she could resist him.

And that was when she gave herself fully over to his kiss. To him. That was when she pushed aside all other thoughts and allowed herself this moment, this night, without worry. This night to indulge in mindless, primal passion the likes of which she'd feared after Las Vegas she would never experience again. The likes of which she might not ever be allowed to experience again after tonight.

But tonight, unlike New Year's Eve, she was clearheaded. There was no liquor in her system to dull her senses, to dim her awareness, to fog her memory, to numb any sensation. Tonight she could truly savor every nuance, every spark Brady lit in her blood.

And savor it she did as he deepened their kiss, as his mouth opened over hers and invited her to do the same so their tongues could meet again in playful abandon.

As if he could read her mind and knew she was his for the taking, he slid one arm under her knees and the other around her back and stood, carrying her with him as his mouth still plundered hers.

He didn't set her down until they'd reached the side of her bed where he let her feet fall to the floor without releasing her from his hold.

By then Kate's arms were around his neck, her hands in his hair, and she was lost in the minuet of his mouth over hers, in the game of hide-and-seek with his tongue, in the feel of his body against her.

His hands went to her back in a massage much like the one he'd done on her legs, arousing, enlivening, easing away all tension, all turmoil, all tiredness.

Those same strong hands rose to her shoulders, slipped over to her collarbone and then came forward, taking both breasts into their magical grip and sending a whole new maelstrom of that glitter all through her.

Her body responded with a will of its own—her back arched, thrusting those ultrasensitive, much-fuller orbs into his palms, her nipples taut and straining and feeling as if they might burst right through her clothes. Clothes she wished would disappear.

With that thought uppermost in her mind, she tore Brady's shirttails from his jeans, not caring that some of the snaps that held it closed popped in the process. In fact, she opted for finishing the job herself to leave his shirtfront open, the ends dangling around his hips.

She plunged her hands inside, pressing her flattened palms up his chest to his shoulders and smoothing the shirt off until it fell to the floor at his feet.

He'd had to leave her breasts to free his arms and, rather than return, he reached around again to lower the zipper of her dress.

Good! Good! Get rid of it! was all she could think

as she rolled her shoulders a little to aid him as he pushed dress, bra and panties down at once.

But he didn't leave her the only one nude for long. Instead his hands went to the button and zipper of his own jeans, making quick work of shedding everything else he had on.

Then he raised his hands to hold her face cradled in them as he kissed her even more deeply, even more soundly, before he abandoned her lips to look down at her body, bare before him, as if it were some rare work of art he were viewing for the first time, something awe inspiring and incredible to behold.

And that was how she felt—genuinely beautiful and not at all bashful or ashamed or embarrassed by her own nudity. How could she be bashful or ashamed or embarrassed by anything that had the ability to affect him so profoundly?

And it did affect him. Kate knew not only from the expression on his handsome face and the deepening of his breathing at just the sight of her, but also because she let her eyes do some roaming of their own—down massive shoulders and carved pectorals to his flat stomach and farther still to the long, thick hardness of his obvious desire for her.

His hands guided her face upward so he could recapture her mouth with his, hungrily, urgently, his lips apart and his tongue thrusting into her mouth to conquer hers, to incite her pulse to race, her blood to run hot in her veins.

Then all at once he stopped again, lying on the bed and pulling her with him to rest beside him even as he rose above her to kiss her, to cup her face with his palm for a moment before sliding it to the side of her neck where he flipped it so that the back of his hand ran down the center of her, between her breasts.

Breasts that were engorged and yearning, with nipples knotted into diamonds of need.

But down, still, went that hand. The backs of his fingers grazing her stomach, veering to her thigh before switching course to retrace the path, this time whispering across one of those kerneled nipples in such torment her spine arched, bringing her inches off the mattress.

That was when he took hold. That warm, strong hand closed around the full globe of her breast, gently at first, then firmly, filling itself with her, letting the crest tense in his palm as he lifted and kneaded and worked wonders so great it made her moan somewhere deep in her soul.

He kissed a similar path down the side of her neck to the hollow of her throat and then farther still, kisses that were like a necklace of glimmering pearls that fell between her breasts before he chose just one breast to take into the warm black velvet of his mouth, drawing it into that moist cavern of delight. His tongue found her nipple, circling it, toying with it, flicking it tip to tip, rolling that incredibly aroused peak between tender teeth until she thought she might pass out from the pure pleasure of it.

But he had so many more gifts to give as his hand began another descent. A slower, ever more tantalizing glide that paused at her middle, exploring the new, resilient curve of her stomach before he continued on, ending between her legs with gentle, seeking fingers that slipped inside her and took her breath away with the wonder of his touch.

Memories of New Year's Eve were fuzzier than she'd realized because never in any mental reliving of that night had anything he'd done felt so incomprehensibly spectacular. Every nerve ending seemed to rise to the surface of her skin, alive and as sparkling as shards of glass.

She needed this man. She wanted him so much it had a life force of its own and she couldn't have fought it if she'd tried.

He came over her then, above her, finessing his way between her thighs, fitting himself into that spot that seemed fashioned for him alone.

Carefully—oh, so carefully—he entered her, giving her her heart's desire in that moment when his body filled her. When his body completed her.

And as he began to move it was a swell she rode, a rise and fall that she answered with her breasts thrust upward, with her arms around him, with her body in harmony and rhythm with his.

Faster and faster he went and she kept pace, striving, straining, yearning for every moment, for every movement that brought them both closer to that pinnacle she'd known only once before.

And when she reached that point, it was nothing like she remembered. It was so much more glorious, as they clung together and climaxed at once. Her fingers dug into Brady's back, her legs wrapped around his, her hips thrust up into him to take him so totally within her that she thought he might actually reach the baby he'd made in her that single time before. White light seemed to erupt within her, white hot light that blinded her to everything but the exquisite rapture and exultation of their united bodies and spirits combined into an immeasurable bliss.

And then the feeling began to ebb. The light. The exquisite pleasure. The ecstasy. Bringing them both back to earth slowly, slowly, leaving Kate feeling sated and languorous and more wonderful than she could ever recall feeling in her life.

Brady's breathing was heavy against her ear as he settled atop her, and she felt his every muscle relax. But he only allowed himself a moment of that before he took his own weight onto himself again by raising up onto his elbows even as his brow came to rest against hers.

"Are you okay? I got carried away."

Kate couldn't help laughing at that because he hadn't been any more carried away than she had. "I'm fine," she assured him. "A whole lot better than fine."

"I didn't hurt…anything?"

"Did you hear me cry out in pain?" she joked.

She felt rather than saw him smile. "I heard you cry out, but it didn't sound like pain."

"Because it wasn't."

He slipped out of her then and rolled to his side,

taking her with him to lie in the lee of his arm, her head on his chest.

"Can I stay the night?" he asked in a passion-raspy voice that was about as sexy as anything she'd ever heard.

"Oh, yes," she breathed against the satin over steel of his pectoral, thinking only that she wouldn't have been able to bear his leaving right then and not taking into consideration the illness she was prone to each morning.

"And we'll worry about tomorrow when it comes?"

She wasn't sure what that meant, but she was too tired to ask. In fact she was so exhausted she couldn't keep her eyes open.

"Tomorrow," she barely managed to murmur before a long sigh escaped her in response to the unadulterated joy of lying there in Brady's arms, cocooned by his big body and bathed in the warmth of his breath as she and his baby fell asleep.

Chapter Twelve

When Brady woke up just before dawn the following morning, he felt as if everything was right with the world. He had a lot on his mind. A whole lot. But Kate was asleep on her side in the curve his body made around hers, and the crystal-clear memory of making love to her was enough to temporarily put a rosy glow on even the deepest of his concerns.

It felt amazing to be in her bed, to be lying the way they were, with her head beneath his chin, her back snuggled against his chest, her small rear end in his lap, and his arm tracing the length of hers so their fingers could be entwined on the pillow in front of her face. It felt so amazing that he didn't want to disturb anything. And he certainly didn't want to leave her.

But he could see the sun beginning to come up through the window, and he knew her brothers would be stirring any minute. He didn't want to meet one of them, coming out of Kate's room. And he also didn't want to risk Kate feeling as panicked as she had New Year's morning at that same thought.

So he kissed the top of her head and eased himself away from her, making sure she was well covered by the sheets and blankets so she would stay warm.

Once he'd pulled on his jeans, he scribbled a quick note on a piece of paper to let her know why he'd left and propped it behind the faucet in the bathroom where she'd be sure to see it.

He gathered up the remainder of his clothes and then debated about whether to leave through the door to the hallway or through the outside door from the sitting room.

He ended up opting for the French doors that led out onto the porch, rather than risk meeting her family, and slipped into the sitting room of his suite next door just as stealthily.

But once he was safely inside again, Kate was still uppermost on his mind.

Not that that was unusual for him lately. She'd held a prominent place there from the moment they'd met. But these last several days with her had left him unable to think about much else. Only now he knew he needed to consider some things he *hadn't* been thinking about. And fast. Things like what his feelings for her were, what was happening between them, where they were headed. Where he wanted

them to be headed. Because now that he thought he
had an idea what was going on with her, he couldn't
just play around.

Play around? Was that what he'd been doing with
her before now? It wasn't, he told himself as he went
through his bedroom into his own bathroom to
shower.

Okay, maybe in Las Vegas, before New Year's
Eve, he'd only been playing. Having a good time.
No strings attached. Falling into some old patterns
with women. Old patterns he'd followed before Claudia. Before Claudia had pulled the rug out from under him.

But getting to know Kate even just a little in Las
Vegas, spending that night with her, had changed
things for him. He just hadn't recognized it before,
because of the way they'd parted that next morning.

But the truth was, the way he'd felt about Kate
then and the way he felt about her now were different
from the way he'd ever felt about anyone else. Different from the way he'd felt about Claudia, even.

With Claudia he'd felt as if he were infected with
something. Something that hadn't always been good,
but that he'd been consumed by nevertheless.

With Kate… Well, he was powerless to control the
feelings she brought alive in him, but none of them
were bad. They were all great. Great enough to have
pushed him to look past her reticence about being
with him. To work to override her hesitations. But
not in a crazed, obsessed mind-set, the way he'd been
after Claudia had rejected him. And not because Kate

had seemed like some kind of challenge he had to conquer.

No, with Kate he hadn't felt the frantic need to please, to win her over, even in view of her reaction New Year's morning. He hadn't felt the kind of desperation he'd felt with Claudia—the things Matt thought had come out of shock at being rejected for the first time in his life.

With Kate he'd felt relaxed and able to be himself. He'd felt calm and content and comfortable.

That sounded very big brotherish, he thought as he soaped himself up.

But big brotherish was definitely not how he'd intended it. Because along with that calmness and contentment and comfort, he'd also been totally churned up over her. He'd wanted her again so much it had nearly hurt.

And that seemed like a pretty terrific combination to him. Certainly it wasn't at all like the desperate determination he'd felt to win Claudia, coupled with the underlying self-disgust that had made him wonder at himself and at what the hell he was doing.

No, his feelings for Kate weren't what he'd felt for Claudia. They weren't what he'd felt in pursuit of Claudia. They weren't tinged with that insanity he believed his feelings for Claudia had been.

In fact, they seemed altogether pretty healthy. Robustly healthy.

But what about Kate's feelings for him?

That thought gave him pause as he rinsed off under the spray of the shower.

As time had passed since his arrival in Elk Creek, and he and Kate had grown closer, he hadn't been worrying as much that she couldn't stand the sight of him, the way he'd been afraid might be the case after New Year's morning. But how much deeper did her feelings go?

He couldn't be sure, and since that rejection still had the power to sting he knew he had to factor it in.

But when he really thought about it, objectively, he decided there were grounds for writing it off to circumstances that didn't reflect on him personally. Because in retrospect Kate's reaction seemed like a fairly natural response to the impromptu wedding and losing her virginity under the influence. He didn't know any woman who wouldn't have been upset, now that he thought about it.

But that still didn't tell him what she *did* feel about him.

What if she was just playing around with *him?*

The very idea of that made him chuckle as he turned off the water and dragged his hands through his hair.

Kate just playing around with him? No, not Kate. She wasn't that kind of woman, and he knew it. She had too much substance, too much character. She wouldn't just play around with anyone on a lark, not with anyone she didn't have feelings for, regardless of what had happened in Las Vegas.

And if she wouldn't play around with anyone she

didn't have feelings for, that must mean that she *did* have feelings for him. Maybe even serious feelings.

Brady stepped out of the shower stall and grabbed a towel to dry off, satisfied with the conclusions he'd come to.

He cared about Kate and thought there was a strong possibility that she cared about him. And that was a good thing.

Because he was also reasonably certain that they were in a pretty delicate position. A delicate position that they were going to have to deal with together.

And the sooner the better, as far as he was concerned.

"You're taking my sister breakfast in bed?"

Kate heard Matt's muted voice coming from the hallway outside her room, and she willed what she was afraid was about to happen, not to.

"I want to talk to her about something. Thought I'd ply her with food, yeah," Brady responded, confirming her worst fears.

She'd only been awake a little over an hour. An hour in which she'd found Brady's note in the bathroom because she'd been in there being sick. And while she would rather have been able to wake up in his arms this morning, she was glad he hadn't been there to watch her make her daily mad dash to the john. She certainly wasn't ready for company yet, though, since the morning sickness was still in its ebb-and-flow cycle, and despite the lull she was in at that moment she knew it could strike again at any time. The last thing she wanted was to have Brady there when it did.

But after that brief exchange in the hall, the knock on her door let her know she was out of luck.

She wanted to call, "Go away," but that would have been rude, so she refrained. Instead she took a brief inventory of her appearance, glad she'd washed her face, brushed her hair up into a curly knot at her crown and put on her dark-blue velvet bathrobe. At least she didn't look as awful as she felt.

When the second knock came she had her hand on the knob and, taking a deep breath, she opened the door. But only a few inches.

"Mornin'," Brady said from the other side, smiling a smile that almost looked sympathetic. Although she didn't know why that should be.

He looked as great as always. Standing tall and straight and strong. Dressed in blue jeans and a crisp white Western shirt. His hair was combed rakishly back and his breathtakingly handsome face was freshly shaven.

But the scent of his aftershave—which she ordinarily liked—didn't help the nausea she knew by then was unstoppable and so rather than return his greeting, she said, "I woke up with another touch of that flu. I'm not up to company."

His expression was unreadable, but his response to her flu excuse was to shake his head in denial. "Let me in, Kate. I brought you tea and toast." He raised the tray he was carrying to prove it. "You can eat or not, but we need to talk."

His tone was part cajoling, part commanding. But it didn't change how she was feeling.

"Honestly, I'm not up to—"

"I know what you're up to," he said, the commanding tone overpowering the cajoling one. "Open the door and let me in."

He knew what she was up to? What did that mean?

A cold clamminess washed over her, even as she told herself he couldn't possibly know *what she was up to.* Maybe he thought she was just spurning him the way she had New Year's morning. Maybe that was what he believed she was "up to."

"I'm really sick, Brady," she said as if that would disabuse him of the notion that what she was doing bore any resemblance to that other morning.

"I know you are. Let me in, anyway."

How did he know she was?

That cold, clammy feeling got worse, and Kate knew what was going to happen as a wave of nausea reared its ugly head.

"Just go away!" she said in a hushed, curt whisper, more worried about fighting down her sick feeling than about imparting the message that this wasn't like New Year's morning.

"No, I won't go away," Brady insisted stubbornly.

But Kate couldn't argue anymore because at that moment she had to turn and run for the bathroom.

Fifteen minutes later, after being ill, brushing her teeth and rinsing her mouth with mouthwash, she walked out of the bathroom to find Brady in her bedroom.

He'd left the tray of tea and toast on the nightstand beside her bed, pulled her desk chair so it was facing the room rather than the corner desk and sat there, one ankle atop the opposite knee, his arms crossed over his chest. Waiting.

"Please go away," she said, calmly now, sounding almost as weak as she felt.

This time Brady didn't even shake his head to address her request. He just stared at her. "How much longer were you going to wait to tell me you're pregnant?" he asked then, in a quiet voice.

For a moment she thought about denying the truth. But what was the point, when she'd been going to break the news to him anytime now, anyway? Besides, she didn't have the strength at that moment to play games, so she just let herself wilt onto the edge of the mattress and, out of curiosity, said, "What makes you think I am?"

He shrugged one of those broad shoulders. "A couple of things," he said matter-of-factly, giving her no clue as to how he felt. "I had a neighbor in Oklahoma who came over to my place on Sunday mornings to fry the sausage he liked for his breakfast because his wife was pregnant and would lose her cookies at just the smell of it—like you did the other night over the rumaki. And then the sickness would pass and she'd be right as rain—just the way you were. Plus there are the changes in your body. Your face and arms and legs are thinner than they were two months ago, but when I touched you... There's more up top, and instead of that flat stomach you had before, there's a little rise.''

''I didn't think you remembered that much about the night in Las Vegas.''

''There are a lot of things that are fuzzy, but I've been dreamin' about that body of yours in vivid, living color ever since—there wasn't anything about you that I didn't remember.''

He didn't seem angry or upset, so it was difficult for Kate to tell what was going on with him. Until it occurred to her that he might not have realized the baby was his.

But just about the time she thought that, he said, ''I did some checkin' with Matt—not so he'd be suspicious, he thought I was just showin' an interest in you—but I know you haven't so much as had a date since we were together. And with my being your first...I know it's mine.''

It...

Somehow that sounded so cold. So removed. So impersonal. So different from how she felt about the baby.

But it was good in a way. It seemed to confirm her every thought about how he'd react—how any man would react to an accidental pregnancy—and it gave Kate a renewed strength in her convictions.

''It doesn't matter,'' she said then.

''It doesn't matter? It sure as hell does matter,'' he said, obviously not appreciating the remark.

''I meant, you don't have to worry that I'll expect

or need anything from you. I've already decided that I want the baby and I'm perfectly capable of raising and supporting it myself, so you can do as you like.''

''What does that mean—I can do as I like?''

''You can be a part of the baby's life—the way any divorced dad is—or you can go on about your business as if the baby isn't even yours. You can even resell the Barton place and leave town if that's what you want to do. I won't hold it against you, and I won't come after you for anything.''

He looked at her as if she were out of her mind. ''What kind of man do you think I am?'' he demanded, his tone full of offense.

She actually did think about what kind of man he was for a moment. Realistically. And in the process she realized why even the suggestion that he would turn his back on the baby would aggravate him.

''You're the kind of man who probably thinks he should do right by me—that's Junebug's turn of phrase. But what I'm telling you is that what that involves can be flexible.''

''I don't know how. I'm the father of this baby and I'm going to *be* the father of this baby. There's no question about it. I've done plenty of playin' in my time, and I always knew that if I got caught at it this way I'd step up and do what needed to be done.''

If he got caught?

If ever Kate had had a doubt about her assumption that he would feel trapped, that statement and the way he'd said it took that doubt away. Caught in the trap of an unplanned baby was what he meant, and she knew it as surely as she was sitting there.

"Understand this—you are not 'caught,'" she said firmly, a little righteous anger of her own sounding in her voice. "You have the option to go on as if this had never happened. I'm not asking anything of you. You can be around or you can not be around. It won't make any difference."

"I can be around or not be around—those are my only choices. Look on from the sidelines or high-tail it out of here?"

"I didn't say anything about only looking on from the sidelines. There can be visitation."

"Visitation."

Why was it that every word she said seemed to strike him wrong? Was he disappointed that she wasn't begging him to make an honest woman of her?

"You can be as much or as little a part of the baby's life as you want. Plain and simple," she re-iterated.

"And what about being a part of your life?"

"Well, we'll be coparents, I guess, if you want to be included in things."

"Coparents. And is that what we've been doin' since I got here? Practicin' to be coparents? Is that what we were doin' in that bed last night?"

She felt as if another of her fears had come to pass. "There wasn't any ulterior motive, if that's what you're thinking. It wasn't a plot to lure you in so I could trap you. I want to be clear about that. Maybe

I got carried away, again, but my friend Kelly says it's because of happy hormones. Something left over from primitive days when women needed the father of their baby to appeal to them so they'd want them around to provide for them. But that's all there was to it, and now that you know about the baby—''

Brady stood up so abruptly, so fiercely, he nearly knocked the chair over. ''You expect me to believe that this was some hormonal thing?''

Okay, so no, it didn't feel like simply some hormonal thing. It felt like a whole lot more. But she wasn't going to admit that. Not in the same conversation in which he'd referred to himself as ''caught.''

''It was a lapse,'' she amended, hoping to make it sound better. ''Like in Las Vegas. There's just some kind of chemistry between us that seems to make us end up in bed. But it didn't have anything to do with anything else. And now that you know about the baby, well, we'll just have to have more restraint. We'll have to be more responsible.''

''How 'bout responsible enough to stay married?''

''*Stay* married?'' Kate repeated. ''You say that as if it was a viable marriage in the first place, when all it really was was a technicality. Besides, the divorce papers are signed and notarized—we're more divorced than married.''

''Not until the papers are filed, we're not.''

''Well I *want* them filed,'' she said forcefully. ''This doesn't change a thing. I don't have any illusions about what a disaster in the making it is for us not to go through with the divorce. Staying married is just asking for a simmering pot of regret and resentment that will boil over and burn everyone in its path. Baby or no baby, papers filed or not filed, you're still free as the breeze as far as I'm concerned."

Even though it made something ache inside her to think about that.

"You said yourself that you're not ready to settle down," she continued. "And I'm telling you that you don't have to. You can go on just the way you planned. You can see the baby, be a part of the baby's life, but you won't have me or the baby as a burden of any kind. I won't be a noose around your neck."

And she wouldn't rely on him the way she'd come to rely on Dwight, either. She wouldn't count on Brady being there for her or for the baby, so if she turned around one day and found him gone, it wouldn't hurt the way it had when Dwight had left her.

"And if I told you I might be falling in love with you?" Brady said then, very, very quietly.

To Kate it sounded like testing the waters, as if he thought if he said that it might convince her to do what some sense of duty or obligation was urging him to do.

"You're only suggesting that because you think you have to, and I'm telling you that you don't. It's just better if we both keep our heads about all this."

"That's very clinical of you. Obviously those

happy hormones aren't clouding your thinking with anything like emotions or feelings for me.''

Kate was suddenly too sick again to argue with him. To tell him she couldn't *let* emotions cloud her thinking.

"Please just go," she said desperately, pressing her fingertips to her mouth as she fought another swell of nausea and some unexpected tears that pooled in her eyes.

"Tell me you don't feel anything for me, Kate," he challenged, rather than leaving the way she wanted him to.

"My feelings aren't the feelings that count. Yours are. The ones that make you feel caught in some trap I never set. And I won't have anything to do with that. Now go!" she nearly shouted, not wanting him to be there through another bout of her illness and especially not wanting him to see her cry, since she was feeling less and less able to stop it.

"So this really is just a replay of New Year's morning," he said more to himself than to her.

Maybe she did sound as shrill as she had then. But she couldn't help it. She knew better than to foster her feelings for Brady, let alone admit to them. Feelings that could cause her to make the wrong decisions. Decisions that would lead her to what they'd led Kelly to. That could lead Brady to hate her. To hate the baby. And she didn't want that.

"Just go!" she said as heartsickness and morning sickness seemed to join forces, and she had to run for the bathroom again.

Chapter Thirteen

Kate didn't leave her rooms that day, and by early evening Matt came looking for her. He knocked on the sitting room door but didn't wait for an invitation to poke his head in.

"Somebody have you tied up in here?" he joked.

Kate was still in her bathrobe. She'd gotten over the morning sickness, as usual, but hadn't had the impetus to get herself dressed. Not after she'd come out of the bathroom and found that Brady had finally taken her at her word and left her room. Because even though it had been what she'd told him to do, she'd still somehow felt as if the world had come crashing down on her.

So she was sitting with her legs curled underneath

her on the overstuffed chair, watching the sunset through her window.

"Are you sick again?" Matt asked before she'd had the chance to answer his first quip.

"This morning, but not anymore," she said because through the whole day of moping and thinking, she had finally come to the conclusion that it was time to tell everyone what was going on.

"Come in," she urged her brother. "I wanted to talk to you, anyway."

"Good, because I want to talk to you, too. What the hell went on in here this morning? I saw Brady bringing you a breakfast tray—of all things—and the next thing I knew, he was moving out."

"He moved out?" Kate responded dimly. She'd heard some sounds from his rooms, but she hadn't thought for a moment that he was packing his bags. In fact, she'd assumed he was still here, and that's why she hadn't left her rooms all day—she'd known she couldn't see him and keep up the facade that she didn't have feelings for him. Not today. Not when she felt as miserable as she ever had in her life, including when Dwight had eloped with someone else.

"What do you mean Brady moved out?" she asked, trying not to let any of her emotions sound in her voice.

"I mean just what I said—he moved out. The Bartons' son sent movers to clear the place out yesterday and the plan was for Brady to stay here while we did some painting and repairs. Then he was going to send for his furniture and move in. No hurry. But one minute I see him headed in here with breakfast, happy as a lark, and two hours later he announces that he's movin' over to the new place now. Today. Without anything done to it and without a stick of furniture in it. He said he has a bedroll he keeps in the plane, he'll sleep in that. And boom! He's gone. I couldn't talk him out of it. He even bit my head off for tryin'. So what the hell happened in here this morning?''

Matt had crossed the room by then and was sitting on the arm of the couch, a frown on his face to go with the accusatory tone in his voice.

Obviously, Brady hadn't told him any of what had happened between the two of them, and Matt was taking his friend's side by default. So the time had come for an explanation.

But Kate didn't find it easy to give, despite her decision to do just that. Especially when she was working so hard not to break down in tears at the thought that Brady had high-tailed it out of here— away from her—as fast as he could. Even though it was something she'd told him to do if he wanted to. She guessed that deep down she just hadn't wanted him to want to.

"I have a lot to tell you, Matt. I just don't know where to start," she finally said.

"At the beginning."

"The beginning was in Las Vegas. Brady and I got a little closer than we let anybody know."

Kate went on to tell her brother what had begun over the New Year's holiday, how she and Brady had indulged in the inebriated impromptu wedding, the resulting pregnancy she'd so recently found out about, along with what had transpired since Brady's arrival in Elk Creek, up to and including this morning's argument.

It took Matt some time for everything to sink in, and his shock was evident in his expression. But once he'd grasped the whole picture, he said, "So when Brady found out you were pregnant he ran out of here?"

Matt's allegiance had suddenly switched to Kate.

But Kate couldn't leave her brother with the wrong impression of his best friend. "No, it wasn't like that. Apparently, he'd figured out I was pregnant before, on his own. He came in here this morning to ask when I intended to tell him. And as for his leaving, well, I didn't order him to pack his bags and get out, but I urged him to go on as if nothing had changed. And when he suggested we not file the divorce papers and stay married, I made it clear I wasn't going along with that no matter what."

"Why would you do that?"

"Why *wouldn't* I do that?" she countered with enough incredulity to match his.

"For crying out loud, Kate, you're *pregnant!*"

"That doesn't make any difference."

"It makes every difference. What were you thinkin'? You're already married to the guy, even if it was through a joke wedding. Why would you send your husband and the father of your baby packin' when you need him most?"

"I don't *need* him," Kate bristled, even as it occurred to her that while it might be true that she didn't *need* Brady, it didn't take away any of the wanting that was still there to torture her.

"Brady doesn't *want* to be married to me," she insisted. "He only offered to stay that way to do the right thing."

"And you said no, leave?" Matt asked with raging disbelief.

"Of course I said no. But I only said for him to leave if he wanted to. That he didn't have to stick around. That even if he did I still wanted the divorce to go through."

Matt shook his head. "You've made such a huge mistake I can't believe it. No wonder he got out of here. He must have felt like he was relivin' Claudia."

"The woman who dumped him."

"Yes the woman who dumped him and left him burned to a crisp. That's why he was tiptoein' around you at first. But it seemed like he'd gotten past it there at the end and was lettin' himself get close to you. And then what do you do? You push him away. Pregnant and all."

Matt was making her angry.

"He would feel trapped, Matt," she said as if he should see that for himself. "You know that. He'd feel trapped just like Buster did. Just like I've heard you and Ry and Shane and Bax say more than once about guys who end up having to marry someone because they've gotten them pregnant. Do you think

I grew up with four brothers and don't know how you all think about these things?''

Matt had the good grace to look shamefaced. ''Ah, Kate, that's just guys talkin'.''

''It is not. Buster wasn't just talk. He hates Kelly, and he's not too much more fond of his own kids. He blames Kelly for every bad thing that happens to him even now. He tells her outright that she ruined his life. Do you think for one minute that's what I want?''

''Brady is not Buster.''

''No, Buster was madly in love with Kelly before she got pregnant. Brady and I were just— Well, I don't know what we were. But I know he isn't madly in love with me, that's for sure. The most he'd say was that he might be falling in love with me—''

''He said that?'' Matt cut in. ''He admitted even in the face of you tellin' him to take a hike that he loved you?''

''It was marginal, believe me.''

''Probably because you were pullin' a Claudia on him at the time. But to even admit that much, then, is a big deal, Kate.''

''It's not a big deal. It's just something he felt he had to say.''

''Brady doesn't say anything because he thinks he has to. And why would he have had to? You were giving him his walking papers—all he *had* to do was take them and leave. It sounds to me like what he was really doin' was trying to get it across to you that he cares about you and wants to stay married to you and be a father to his baby without going too far out on the limb you were already sawing off.''

"So everything's my fault?" Kate said, her temper flaring more and more.

"A lot of this is, yeah. You said yourself that he knew you were pregnant before this morning. What did he do with that information? Did he run while he still could have without you or anybody else knowing why? No, he stuck around.''

He stuck around and made love to her....

But Kate didn't say that, she just let her brother rant on.

"Then he brings you breakfast in bed to talk about the situation, puttin' himself in my sights when I caught him at it and not carin'. He tells you he loves you—''

"Marginally," Kate reminded, feeling as if they'd both reverted back to bickering kids.

"Marginally or not, he let you know he has feelings for you. He tells you he wants to stay married to you, and you still kick him to the curb.''

"Thanks for understanding, Matt," Kate said facetiously.

Matt ignored her tone. "Why the hell would he have felt trapped when you made it clear he could turn his back if he wanted to and he let you know he didn't want to? That's not being trapped, that's makin' a choice. The same choice I'd make if it was Jenn and me in your situation. Happily.''

"You're already engaged to Jenn and you're crazy about her. The sun rises and sets in her where you're concerned. But Brady was only thinking to do what was right, not what he wanted to do, and certainly not *happily*. He'd be settling, and eventually he'd regret that. He'd resent it. He'd resent me and the baby. He'd look at me and he'd realize he'd been trapped by the world's most resistible woman!''

That last part had come out on its own as part of the full head of steam she'd worked up by the end of what she'd been saying. She regretted it because it revealed too much of what she'd been feeling since Dwight's elopement. Too much of a portion of her that was so vulnerable she was afraid to let it out into the light.

But Matt caught it and wouldn't let go. ''So you still have some baggage of your own that's playing a role in this?''

''Why don't you just go away, Matt. You're not helping anything,'' she blurted out in a fit of temper.

But again her brother ignored her. ''Oh, Kate,'' he said on a sigh, apparently not caring that she hadn't confirmed his opinion. ''Brady was tryin' to put his baggage behind him, but you let yours ruin things.''

''That's not true,'' she defended feebly.

''Bull. You're so busy protecting yourself from the kind of hurt you had when Dwight left you in the dust that you aren't seeing what's right in front of your face.''

''I see what's right in front of my face perfectly clearly every time I picture Kelly.''

''But Brady isn't Buster,'' Matt repeated. ''And

how could Brady feel trapped if he's getting what he wants?''

"It isn't what he wants.''

"I think you are.''

"Well you'd be wrong.''

"That's good, dig in your heels. Don't give him a chance. Take not only your past but Kelly's past and present, too, and pull it all around you like a coat of armor. See what it gets you. It won't be what you want. It won't be what I'm betting Brady wants. It won't be what's best for your baby. But, hey, what difference does that make?''

"Sometimes I wish I were an only child.''

"Sure, push everybody away. It's safer like that, isn't it?''

"Matt…'' she said in the same warning tone she'd used when they were kids and he was going too far in his teasing of her.

"Don't blow it, Kate,'' he said anyway, not heeding the warning. "Brady's a good man. I've watched the way he's been with you since he got here. I've seen the way he looks at you. Things could work out with him. If you let them.'' Matt stood then, his hands on his hips, frowning down at her. "Get your rear end over to the Bartons' place and talk to him. *Listen* to him. And quit puttin' the past and other people's problems between you. Just look at him for what he is.''

Matt left without waiting for a reply, and Kate sank farther into her chair, as if willing it to swallow her alive so she didn't have to deal with any of what her brother had said. With any of what she was feeling.

But the chair didn't swallow her alive.

And like it or not, she couldn't disregard what Matt had said, even if she did go on trying to disregard what she was feeling.

She'd never been more confused.

What if her brother was right? she kept asking herself.

A lot of what he'd said seemed to have some validity. After all, he'd known Brady much longer than she had. So was she seeing her past and Kelly's problems when she looked at Brady and her own situation rather than seeing Brady as Brady?

It was just so hard to say for sure.

She knew she was afraid of reliving that past, afraid of ending up in the same kind of mess Kelly had ended up in—that was a given. She certainly knew she was afraid that Brady would feel trapped by a woman he came to see the way Dwight had seen her—as a woman so resistible Dwight had had no problem maintaining years of celibacy with her and then had turned around and been propelled by such a burning desire for someone else that he'd eloped with her.

And, yes, she guessed that qualified as baggage.

But it was also what had happened, so she believed she had cause to worry. To more than worry. She had cause to be paralyzed with self-doubt.

She knew what Kelly would say to that, though. And what Matt would say to it, too. That obviously

Brady hadn't found her resistible or she wouldn't be pregnant. That if he'd found her resistible he wouldn't have been rooting around the way he had been since getting to Elk Creek. He wouldn't have made love to her again just last night.

And Kate wanted to believe that. She honestly did. It just wasn't easy. Besides, even if it were true now and had been true in Las Vegas, what if it wasn't true for the long haul? Buster had found Kelly irresistible before he'd had to marry her, but afterward he'd hardly touched her—something that had been a huge blow to her friend's self-esteem, too.

Brady isn't Buster....

Kate heard Matt's words in her head as clearly as if he were there to repeat them himself.

But Brady was a man. A man like her brothers, who had all talked that "trapped" talk. A man who had referred to himself as "caught."

Forgetting about that was as difficult as trying to let go of her own sense that she was ultimately resistible.

And how could she discount such thoughts when he'd told her himself that having a wife and a baby right now were not part of his plans? How could she even entertain the notion that he wouldn't look at a forced change in those plans without regret and resentment?

Although, truthfully, Matt was right. She wasn't forcing Brady. She'd opened the door for him. And, yes, she'd probably urged him out of it with enough vigor to remind him of that other woman's rejection.

But, still, he might well have suggested they stay married out of a sense of duty. And if that was the case it would result in the same things, wouldn't it—regret and resentment?

She thought it would.

On the other hand she could be wrong about everything. Wrong about Brady. And Matt could be right when he said that Brady might feel the way Matt would if he and Jenn were in the same situation—that he'd be only too happy about it.

Okay, so a part of her wanted to believe that. Who wouldn't?

But what if it were true? What if that's what Brady would have said if she'd given him half a chance?

Temptation washed through her. Temptation to go to Brady the way Matt had told her to, to give him more of an opportunity to talk than she had this morning. To listen to him without letting her own baggage get in the way.

But should she do that? Was she only looking for an excuse to see him again? An excuse to hang on to hopes she shouldn't hang on to?

That was a hard question to answer. Because after a day of misery she knew she *wanted* an excuse to believe things could work out. She wanted it more than she'd ever wanted anything in her life.

So maybe you should take your brother's advice and go to Brady, hear him out, a little voice in the back of her mind suggested. *Would that be such a mistake?*

Possibly not. Because if she listened very closely,

very carefully, then one way or another she'd know what was really on his mind. Even if it was what she was most afraid of, what she'd already assumed he was thinking. And if what he had to say wasn't enough to convince her he genuinely did want to try to make their marriage work, if it wasn't enough to make her believe his feelings for her—and only for her—were behind it, then she could still make sure the divorce went through....

Kate finally got up from the easy chair and headed to her bedroom to get dressed.

"I hope you're right, Matt," she muttered to herself.

Because if Brady was only thinking in terms of duty or obligation she would still have to turn her back on him.

Only, she wasn't too sure how she could bear to do that again....

There was no welcoming porch light when Kate got to the Bartons' place. Brady's place now. But the front door was open, and a dim glow came through the screen from a fire she could see burning in the fireplace in the living room.

Wondering why Brady would have left the front door open when it was so cool outside, Kate got out of her car and started for the house. She was craning for sight of him through the screen when his deep whisky voice came from the shadows at the far side of the porch.

"What are you doin' here?"

She jumped with fright and stopped dead in her tracks rather than climb the stairs, refocusing her eyes to find him. "You scared me to death," she said, holding a flattened hand to her heart, which was beating faster even than it had been with the tension that had kept her company on the drive over.

Brady didn't apologize. He didn't say anything at all, apparently letting his initial question stand.

Kate took a bolstering breath and climbed the steps to the porch, finding him sitting with one hip atop the railing, his back against a support pillar. He had a bare foot riding the railing, too, so his bent knee could prop a single arm. His other foot was on the porch floor and his left hand was jammed into the pocket of his jeans.

He wore a chambray shirt, but it was open down the front, the tails flying like flags at half-mast around his hips, and he looked as sexy as she'd ever seen him.

Which, for no reason she could name, inspired an image in her mind of him pulling on his clothes after a romp with some female company he might have escorted out only moments before her arrival.

Kate's stomach lurched at the thought, and before she could get control of her own responses she said, "Did I just miss someone?"

"Who would you have just missed?" he asked in a not particularly friendly tone.

"I don't know. You just look...I don't know," she stammered.

"I was workin' on this place all day. I took a

shower to clean myself up and came out here to cool off."

Relief was a living thing inside her, even though Kate felt like a fool for what she'd been thinking. Of course, his explanation made more sense.

"Is that why you came over here? To check up on me?" he asked then, almost as if he'd known what she'd been imagining.

"No," she said quickly, quietly.

"Then why are you here?"

Kate mentally called upon some badly needed courage and said, "I had a chat with Matt a little bit ago. A pretty heated chat. I told him everything."

"And you came to warn me to head for the hills before all four of your brothers come to string me up?"

"I'm who Matt's disgusted with," she said into the shadows as a shiver shook her voice in an involuntary reaction to the cold that was seeping in through the denim jacket, crew-neck T-shirt and jeans she had on.

Brady seemed to notice the shiver because he came off the railing and said, "Let's go inside."

There was only a hint of concern in his tone, but Kate held on to it hopefully. Maybe if he cared that she was cold he cared about her.

He went ahead of her to the door, opening the screen and waiting for her to go in.

Kate didn't hesitate to step into the warmth of the living room. She made a beeline for the fireplace and the heat it was giving off, stopping only a few feet from the hearth as Brady followed, closing the door behind them to shut out the chill.

He ended up at the fireplace, too, standing with an arm braced on the mantel so he could see her face. His weight was slung onto his right hip in a way that made the side of his shirt fall away from his body, so that his expansive chest was gilded by the golden illumination of the dancing flames below.

"What's Matt disgusted with you about? Sleepin' with me?" Brady asked then.

Kate dragged her gaze off the delectable sight of his naked torso so she could concentrate on the conversation.

"No. My brother gave me what-for for doing more talking than listening this morning. He said it sounded like I didn't give you a chance."

"You didn't."

"He said I let my own baggage get in the way and probably reminded you of yours in the process."

"Smart guy, your brother."

"So I came for a do-over."

Brady watched her intently, his blue-gray eyes boring into her so fiercely she was afraid he was going to just tell her it was too late, that he'd given her her only opportunity this morning.

But instead he said, "I didn't handle things too well myself. I expected you to jump at the idea of stayin' married. And when you didn't—"

"Matt said I 'pulled a Claudia.'"

"I had some flashbacks, yeah."

"I'm sorry."

"I just want to know how much like Claudia this morning was," he said in a gruff voice that let her know she really had scratched old wounds.

"How much like her I was?" she repeated, unsure what he was asking.

"I thought she had feelings for me and she didn't."

Ahh...

"I'm not like her at all in that area," Kate admitted, her voice quiet once again, because she knew she was venturing out onto a limb of her own.

But that didn't seem to be enough for him, because he just stood there, watching her as if he were waiting for her to say more.

"This isn't easy for me, Brady," she blurted out. "I have this friend—my best friend—and she got pregnant just out of high school. The father was the love of her life. They were planning to get married after college, but when she got pregnant and they couldn't wait, everything changed. It's been horrible for both of them and for the twins they had, ever since. The marriage ended in divorce. He says she ruined his life. He hates her. I didn't want to end up like that. I didn't want *us* to end up like that. And when I factored in that I'm a person who my ex-fiancé didn't find attractive enough to be in any hurry to get into bed, along with a lot of guy talk I've heard over the years from my brothers about men getting trapped, and then you saying yourself that you were caught... Well, I just thought it was better for everybody to cut you loose, no matter how I felt about you."

He didn't say anything for the longest time, and it was very unnerving for her. Especially in light of the fact that she'd just opened herself up so completely to him. And all Kate could think was that maybe she'd poured her heart out to a man who didn't care. Who maybe didn't even like her. A man who maybe she *should* turn and run from before she embarrassed herself any more.

Then he said, "You really do have baggage," as if it were all inconsequential now that it had been aired.

"I just wanted you to see that I wasn't 'pulling a Claudia' this morning and rejecting you. I thought I was giving you what you—or any other man—would want by not asking or expecting anything from you. By making sure you knew that you were still free in spite of the baby." Kate stopped herself from going on, realizing that once again she was doing all the talking. "I'm not saying anything else. I came to listen."

Brady nodded and went on watching her awhile longer before he finally said, "The first thing I better tell you is that I burned the divorce papers in this fire when I started it tonight."

"You did?"

"I decided today that I wasn't lettin' you go. I just hoped to hell I wasn't doin' what I did with Claudia. I've been hopin' to hell all along that that wasn't what I was doin'."

"What did you do with her?"

"I made a fool of myself chasin' after her. I didn't want to make the same mistake with you—chasin' after you after Las Vegas when you let me know in no uncertain terms that I was your biggest nightmare."

Kate flinched. "You were a long way from my biggest nightmare. I just couldn't believe what I'd done."

"Yeah, I came to that conclusion myself. That's why I thought we had a shot at makin' this work out. Till you made yourself clear this mornin'."

"I just—"

"I know what you *just*. But you're wrong. I was crazy about you from the start, Kate. Do you really think that if you hadn't acted as if you wanted to shoot me New Year's morning I wouldn't have gladly let all your brothers know I was interested in you? I hadn't been hidin' anything before that. I agreed to keep everything secret because that was how you wanted it and because no, I wasn't wild about the idea of lettin' them know we'd had what you were determined was only going to be a one-night stand and that after that one-night stand you wanted nothin' to do with me. Keepin' that from your brothers was purely an act of survival. But if you hadn't insisted on things bein' hushed up, or gettin' away from me that morning, it would have only been the beginning for us."

"It would have?"

"You remember when I told you about my father

never giving up until he'd won over my mother? And you asked me if that was the kind of love I was lookin' for? Well, I'd never thought about it before, but you were right. And the thing is, you're it. Pregnant or not pregnant—you're it. You were it from the minute I set eyes on you in Las Vegas. I just didn't realize it until I sorted through everything in my head today.

"Yeah, maybe a little of this morning was me doin' the right thing. But after a day of scrubbin' this place from stem to stern and spendin' all that time thinkin' about nothin' but you, I can stand here now and tell you without a doubt that I'm in love with you, Kate McDermot. That even if there was no baby, I'd still be in love with you. I'd still want you to stay my wife. That's why I burned the divorce papers—because no matter what you said New Year's morning, no matter what you said this morning, I figured I was goin' by your actions instead, and you didn't act like somebody who didn't want me."

Okay, so maybe she owed Matt a big kiss.

"I don't act like somebody who doesn't want you because I'm *not* somebody who doesn't want you."

"Meanin' you *do* want me?"

Kate nodded because her throat was suddenly constricted with too many tears to answer him.

"I'm in love with you, Kate," he repeated, just in case she hadn't caught it the first time.

"I'm in love with you, too, Brady," she whispered, because it was the most she could manage.

"And I'm not givin' you a divorce. Not now. Not ever. You're my wife and you're stayin' my wife. If that makes *you* feel trapped then that's just too damn bad."

She could only laugh at that as the tears flooded her eyes and ran down her face.

Seeing them made Brady push away from the mantel and close the space between them.

"What're these for?" he asked, wiping the moisture with a gentle thumb at each cheek.

"I love you," was her only response.

"I more than love you," he said. "I want you so much it's like a thirst I can't quench."

He took her into his arms then, kissing both damp cheeks before his lips pressed to hers in that way that was familiar now but that she still knew she would never get enough of.

And that was all it took for sparks to fly between them. For hunger to be awakened and passion to ignite. Passion greater than either of the other times they'd made love.

Kate wasn't sure if it was because this was the first time they'd come together with love stated and out in the open, knowing they had an unbreakable bond, a commitment to each other, but something made her feel more free, more uninhibited, more able to savor every kiss, every caress, every movement of his hands on her.

Clothes were shed in a hurry and they lay down on the floor in front of the fire, too much in need of bare flesh pressed to bare flesh to even seek out Brady's bedroll.

His mouth was everywhere. His hands were everywhere. And the driving desire he orchestrated in her body was like nothing she'd ever felt before— hot and wild and demanding.

When he slipped inside her, she was more than ready. Her back arched and a groan of the purest pleasure rolled from her throat. Deeply, deeply inside her was the staff of life, driving them both in a relentless climb up a mountain of delight to a pinnacle that flamed into an inferno, leaving Kate clinging to Brady as she called his name in that moment of sublime ecstasy that made her spirit soar with his, that truly joined them.

And when it was over and he eased them both back to earth, Kate had a second surprise in the sense of joy that filled her—body and soul—with the knowledge that this man loved her. That they would have a whole lifetime of what she felt they'd just discovered in each other.

After a few minutes of calming his breathing, Brady took one more full breath and then exhaled in a replete sigh and rolled to his side. He left one arm under her head and his body half covering her, his thigh a wonderful weight across her lap.

"We have to do this more than three times in almost as many months," he said as he relaxed.

Kate laughed. "The way I look at it we've done it twice in less than twenty-four hours."

"That's more like it. We'll just have to keep *that* up."

"I'm game if you are," she said with a little nudge into the juncture of his legs at her hip.

"Just give me a few minutes," he said wryly, bestowing a sweet kiss full of promise before he abandoned her lips again.

"So Matt knows we're married," Brady said then, resting his head beside hers on his arm.

"And he's probably told everyone else by now."

"Good, then they won't think anything about you not comin' home tonight."

"And after tonight?" she asked, testing the waters.

"After tonight you can choose—we can stay here and live like Bohemians, or we can stay at your ranch until we get this place in order and furnished and can move in properly."

Kate thought about how comfortable she was, just lying on the floor with nothing but Brady's arm as her pillow, his body as her blanket, and she knew she didn't really need anything more than that.

"Let's stay here," she said, eager to dive right into their life together.

"Good choice," he said, kissing her temple this time. "I do love you, Kate," he added then. "Forget about that Dwight guy not wanting you. I want you enough for both of us. And I want this baby, too. Enough to surprise the hell out of me."

"You're sure?"

"More sure than I've ever been about anything except how much I love you."

"Good thing," she said with a laugh as his hand played at her stomach, exploring the slight changes the baby had made there already.

Kate smiled up into the face she loved so much it was almost an ache inside her, pressing a palm to his cheek as if only touching him could convince her that he was real. That his love for her was real. That the life they would have together was real.

That was when he rose above her again, recapturing her mouth with his, caressing her with those wonderful hands, nudging a knee between her thighs.

And as Kate felt arousal spring back to life once more, she knew she was right where she belonged. Right where she and their baby belonged.

With Brady.

Forever with Brady.

*   *   *   *   *

Look for Victoria Pade's

FROM BOSS TO BRIDEGROOM,

part of Silhouette's
original continuity series,
THE COLTONS,
on sale in October 2001.

Don't miss this exciting new Silhouette Special Edition series from Laurie Paige!

Twenty years ago, tragedy struck the Windoms. Now the truth will be revealed with the power—and passion—of true love! Meet Kate, Shannon and Megan, three cousins who vow to restore the family name.

THE WINDRAVEN LEGACY

On sale May 2001
A stranger came, looking for a place to stay— but what was he really looking for…? Find out why Kate has **SOMETHING TO TALK ABOUT.**

On sale July 2001
An accident robbed Shannon of her sight, but a neighbor refused to let her stay blind about her feelings…in **WHEN I SEE YOUR FACE.**

On sale September 2001
Megan's memories of childhood had been lost. Now she has a chance to discover the truth about love…**WHEN I DREAM OF YOU.**

Available at your favorite retail outlet.

Silhouette®
TM *Where love comes alive*™

Meet 50 loving dads in

babies & BACHELORS USA

Take 4 FREE BOOKS, Plus get a FREE GIFT!

Babies & Bachelors USA is a heartwarming new collection of reissued novels featuring 50 sexy heroes from every state who experience the ups and downs of fatherhood and find time for love all the same. All of the books, hand-picked by our editors, are outstanding romances by some of the world's bestselling authors, including Stella Bagwell, Kristine Rolofson, Judith Arnold and Marie Ferrarella!

**Don't delay, order today! Call customer service at
1-800-873-8635.
Or
Clip this page and mail it to The Reader Service:**

In U.S.A.
P.O. Box 9049
Buffalo, NY
14269-9049

In CANADA
P.O. Box 616
Fort Erie, Ontario
L2A 5X3

YES! Please send me four FREE BOOKS and FREE GIFT along with the next four novels on a 14-day free home preview. If I like the books and decide to keep them, I'll pay just $15.96* U.S. or $18.00* CAN., and there's no charge for shipping and handling. Otherwise, I'll keep the 4 FREE BOOKS and FREE GIFT and return the rest. If I decide to continue, I'll receive six books each month—two of which are always free—until I've received the entire collection. In other words, if I collect all 50 volumes, I will have paid for 32 and received 18 absolutely free!

267 HCK 4534
467 HCK 4535

Name	(Please Print)		
Address		Apt. #	
City	State/Prov.	Zip/Postal Code	

* Terms and prices subject to change without notice.
Sales Tax applicable in N.Y. Canadian residents will be charged applicable provincial taxes and GST. All orders are subject to approval.

DIRBAB01R

© 2000 Harlequin Enterprises Limited

▼ Silhouette® —

where love comes alive—online...

eHARLEQUIN.com

your romantic life

─Romance 101──────
♥ Guides to romance, dating and flirting.

─Dr. Romance ─────
♥ Get romance advice and tips from
our expert, Dr. Romance.

─Recipes for Romance ──
♥ How to plan romantic meals for you
and your sweetie.

─Daily Love Dose────
♥ Tips on how to keep the romance
alive every day.

─Tales from the Heart──
♥ Discuss romantic dilemmas with other
members in our Tales from the Heart
message board.

All this and more available at
www.eHarlequin.com
on Women.com Networks

SINTL1R

SILHOUETTE®
MAKES YOU
A STAR!

Look in the back pages of
all June Silhouette series books to find an
exciting new contest with fabulous prizes!
Available exclusively through Silhouette.

Don't miss it!

Silhouette®
Where love comes alive™

P.S. Watch for details on how you can meet
your favorite Silhouette author.

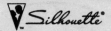

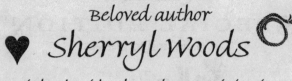

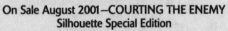
 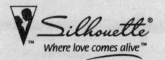